STRANDED IN SNOW SHOE

THE PREQUEL TO SUMMER OF TWO WORLDS

WRITTEN BY:
J. ARTHUR MOORE

ISBN: 978-1-952874-68-0 (softcover)
978-1-952874-69-7 (hardcover)
978-1-952874-70-3 (eBook)

This is a work of fiction with minor historic reference in regard to the Northern Pacific Railroad in North Dakota Territory. The setting of the story is pure fiction and does not exist anywhere in West Virginia, as is the story itself. However, cultural references of the time period of the story are researched for accuracy.

Printed by:

OB OMNIBOOK Co.

OMNIBOOK CO.
99 Wall Street, Suite 118
New York, NY 10005 USA
+1-866-216-99652
www.omnibookcompany.com

design by Gian Carlo Tan
photo editing by Allen E. Miller, Jr.

For e-book purchase: Kindle on Amazon, Barnes and Noble
Wholesale purchase: Ingram (615) 793-5000, Baker & Taylor (800) 775-1800
Book purchase: Amazon.com, Barnes & Noble.com, www.jarthurmoore.com
and www.omnibookcompany.com/journeyintodarkness/

Omnibook titles may be purchased in bulk for educational, business, fund-raising, or sales promotional use. For more information please e-mail info@omnibookcompany.com

Artwork

All illustrative material – photographs, maps, drawings – are by the author, with one exception, the Virginia and Truckee logo seen below. Cover photograph and portrait of Scot were taken at Fairmount Park in Philadelphia, Pennsylvania. Scot Robinson is represented by Eric Malave, a student of the author's at the time. Hank Fillmore is represented by Henry [Hank] Funk, a longtime friend of the author's. His portrait was taken in a period photo studio, the name not on the photo copy in the author's possession. Jeremy Baker is represented by Colton Zawadzki, a visitor at one of the author's events who likes history and character impersonation. His image was captured at Landis Valley Farm Museum in Landis Valley, Pennsylvania. Additional characters are portrayed by the Wunderlich brothers: Andy as Jason Johnston, Paul as Adam Tyler, and James as Brett Tompkins. These boys and their mother are currently a key part of the author's team in the presentation of Civil War living history. Their images were taken at Hopewell Furnace National Historic Site.

AUTHOR'S NOTE

Contrary to common practice, names which this author uses in the series of stories which take place along or are related to the Virginia and Truckee Railroad in West Virginia, do have meaning.

The setting itself grew out of the author's hobby of model railroading and is in part duplicated in miniature recreations. There is, however, a real railroad of the same name and period located in the state of Nevada near Virginia City.

Most of the names of places and characters are from real people and places in the author's experience as a middle grades school teacher, or from places and friends who have been a part of the author's life experiences. All have been chosen from good memories and are a way of saying, "I haven't forgotten you, though we haven't seen each other in years and may never meet again."

Often main characters are created for specific people and stories are dedicated to those individuals. Yet in a sense all the stories which are created as a part of the Virginia and Truckee collection are dedicated to life's memories and the people who have been a part of those memories.

DEDICATION

During the summer of 1979, I spent the summer on staff at Camp Good News, located on Cape Cod in Massachusetts. My invaluable assistant during that summer was a boy named Scot Robbins. In the year that followed I began a story as a remembrance of that time, creating a character named for and as a gift to him, Scot Robinson, stranded in a West Virginia mountain town in search of his uncle. This is that story. Because Scot Robins was not available for a character photograph, Scot Robinson is represented by Eric Malave, a student of the author's in another time and another place.

In a conversation with a close friend at the time of the story's creation, the character of the boy's uncle took shape. That character, Henry [Hank] Fillmore also known as "Horrible Hank", is dedicated to that friend.

Stranded in Snow Shoe is dedicated in His love and the love of friendship to Scot Robins, Eric Malave, Henry [Hank] Funk, Colton Zawadzki, and Andy, James, and Paul Wunderlich.

In memorium
Henry [Hank] Tome Funk
November 15, 1933 – May 25, 2018

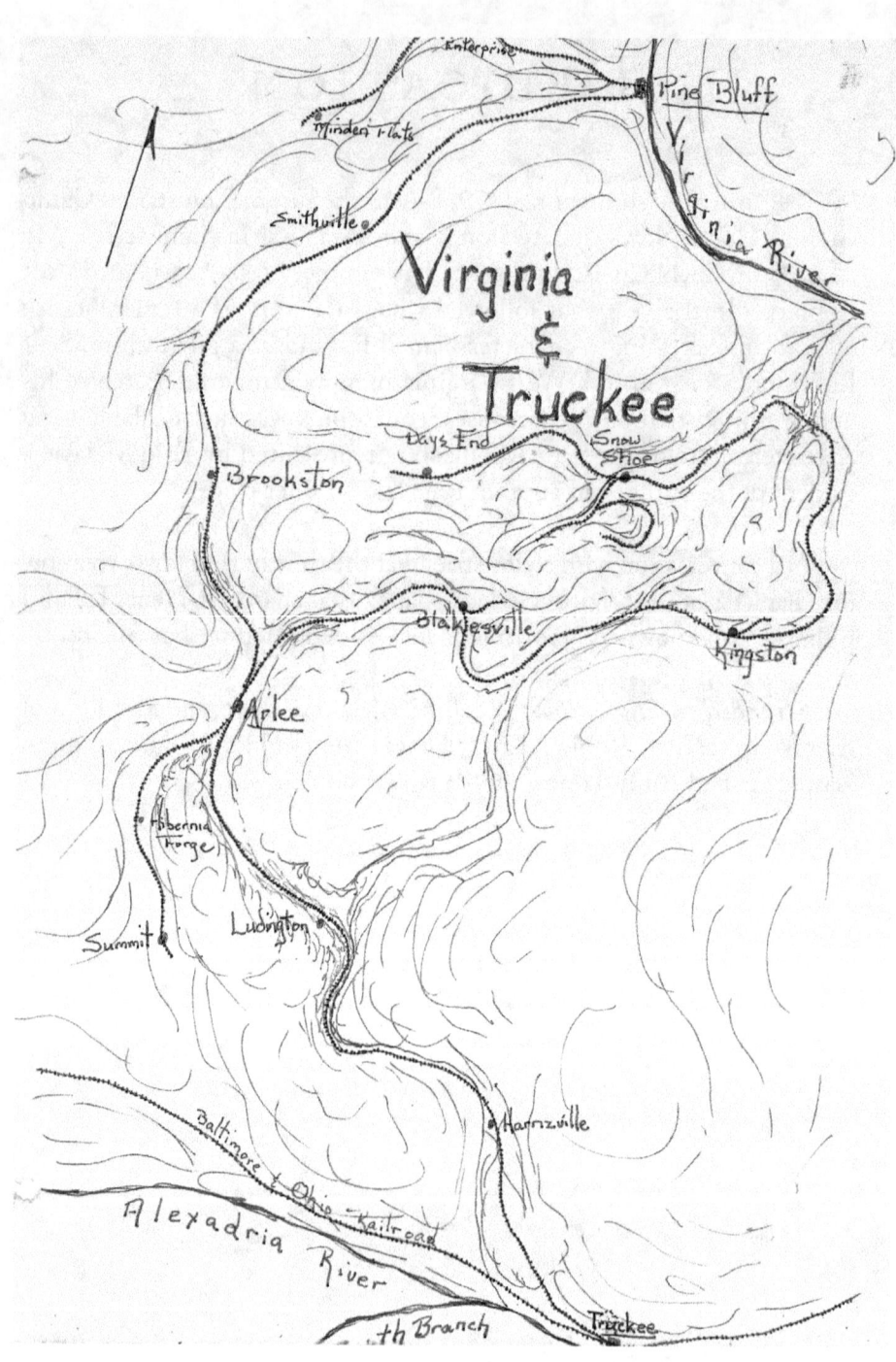

Scot Robinson

HANK FILLMORE

JEREMY BAKER

JASON JOHNSTON

BRETT TOMPKINS

Adam Tyler

Patches of dust floated gently in the early morning rays of sunlight slanting through the east windows of the station room. Bright squares of light heightened the grain in the wooden floorboards where the beams of sun struck, casting sharp shadows from the chair backs of the captain's chairs spotted near the stove. The station room was quiet in the early hours of an early April midweek morning prior to the arrival of the coach run from Arlee. On the other side of the ticket counter, Robert Coates, the station master, was thumbing through a file drawer for the day's freight schedule. He pulled out the needed file and pushed the drawer closed as he turned to walk around his oak desk toward the swivel chair behind. The chair squeaked as the man's weight settled.

Robert Coates was of light build. He stood less than six feet tall. Wire rimmed glasses were worn most of the time, though he occasionally set them aside when he wasn't reading. In his early thirties, he had an abundance of blond hair which he kept neatly trimmed and combed, parted in the middle and swept back behind his ears.

A light clattering of feet descended the stairs and approached from the inner hall. Mr. Coates looked up from his work as Jarrett and Carry entered, lunch kettles in hand. Jarrett, fourteen years old, waited while his nine-year-old sister went around to their father and reached up on tiptoe to kiss him good-bye, before leaving for her job at the millinery shop.

"See ya later, Pa," the boy greeted as he left for his job at the gun shop.

"Bye, Son. Ya have a good day, Carry," the man returned.

"I love ya, Pa," Carry said.

"Me, too, Honey. Now run along 'fore yer late. Have a good day." He watched as the two ran across the office to leave by the far door, which stood open to let in the cool morning air.

"Bye," they waved as they disappeared onto the platform and cut across the tracks toward Railroad Avenue by way of the hardware storage yard.

Returning his thoughts to the work at hand, the station master began to make up the car list for the morning freight run to Arlee. The clock on the wall chimed the half hour. From the west end of town a steam whistle's shrill call announced the departure of the first run of the logging company's train up Fisher Mountain to South Camp. Jamie Rhodes would be checking in shortly to walk the track to Chamber's Crossing where he met the coach from Arlee each morning.

The stationmaster concentrated on car bills at hand. The saw mill had two cars of new lumber for delivery in Pine Bluff and Arlee. There would also be outgoing traffic from Graham Barrel Works, C. H. Ankney Millwork, and empties from Fox Hardware Enterprises, and the Sampson and May Feed and Grain Company. On down the line, cars would be waiting for pickup at Kingston and Blakesville. In all there were twelve cars to be scheduled out.

The quiet was broken by Jamie's cheerful greeting. "Mornin', Mr. Coates."

"Howdy, Jamie." The station master leaned back in his chair. "Care fer coffee before ya head out."

"Thank ya, Sir. But it's such a nice day I'll leave early and take my time. See ya later."

The youth waved as he exited onto the front platform and turned east toward Arlee. The man watched him through the window until he was lost from sight around the bend, then turned back to his desk to finish the freight assignments.

By the time the station clock struck the half hour after nine, the station room had become active with the arrival of outgoing passengers for Day's End and others who had come to meet incoming passengers from the train. Mr. Coates checked his watch against the clock. Glancing through the window, he checked for the column of smoke that would signal the train's approach. At first the horizon was clear. He looked again as he emerged onto the station platform. The train was there. Mr. Coates turned toward the freight room doors where the baggage wagon stood loaded. He wheeled the wagon to the edge of the platform near the tracks.

The train rounded the bend into view. The whistle sounded its shrill call as it approached on the station pass track. The bell began to ring rhythmically as engine Number Twenty-one passed the water tower and slowed for the stop. Pounding pistons slowed, brakes squealed, then a rush of air set the brakes as a blast of steam released the pressure on the steam cylinders. The train stood in the station and the noise of voices filled the air as people began to disembark and the baggage door was rolled open to exchange parcels and personal baggage and the mail.

"Mornin', Rob," Anthony, the baggage clerk, greeted from the open door.

"Mornin', Anthony," the station master returned. "How was the trip up?"

"Routine. Nothin' of interest to report."

The two worked quickly. The wagon was emptied, then piled again with an assortment from within the car. The job completed, the door was rolled closed again. At the coach, the new arrivals had descended to the platform and were preparing to gather their belongings and go their various ways as departing passengers boarded the train.

"All aboard!" the conductor called.

The engineer responded with two blasts on the whistle as steam surged through the pistons and the train rolled forward, easing out of the station and returning to the main line.

Mr. Coates reached for the wagon's tongue, backed his weight away from it, and pulled it across to the freight room. The man paused to rest before unloading.

"Mister?" The voice caught him by surprise. "Could ya tell me where I might find Mr. Hank Fillmore?" A boy of about thirteen stood with a carpet bag in his hand.

"Can't say as I know the name, Boy. Who might be lookin' for him?"

"Name's Scot Robinson. He's my uncle. My folks said I was ta meet him here in Snow Shoe. Said he worked for a loggin' company." Scot put the bag down and pushed some strands of his brown hair back from his eyes. He looked around far a place to sit and found a trunk near the baggage door. He perched himself on its curved top and leaned back against the wall.

The station master scratched the back of his head and rubbed the back of his neck as he tried to recall anyone by the name the boy sought.

"I'm sorry, Scot, but I don't ever recall a body by that name. I do know the man who runs the loggin' company, but he won't be down from the mountain 'til evenin'. Yer welcome ta stay 'round here till then and I'll take ya to him."

"Thanks, Sir," the boy smiled somewhat sadly.

"My name's Coates. I'm station master here."

"Can I be of help, Mr. Coates?" Scot's brown eyes glistened moist as he stood up. He was of average height and of slim but sturdy build. He seemed used to manual work. The man saw callouses on the boy's hands and a firmness in his muscles. But he was drawn to the sadness of those brown eyes and a ready smile they did not share.

Scot helped unload the wagon and sort packages according to customers. During the course of the morning several of the customers stopped by to claim their parcels. The train returned after about a quarter hour and was parked on the track behind the station. The boy watched the crew uncouple the engine and leave for the yard. A second locomotive, Number forty-six, pulled out a previously assembled consist of two carloads of lumber with a caboose at the back end, and located it on the main in front of the station. It then proceeded to assemble the outgoing cars from the various businesses. Scot helped put the way bill board together which Mr. Coates had organized at his desk earlier. The morning load came down off the mountain -- ten cars of logs pushed by the company locomotive. The loaded cars were delivered to the saw mill and the locomotive returned with ten empties and headed to the company main for the return trip to the logging camp. The station master invited the boy to join him for dinner.

* * *

The freight pulled out at mid day. During the early part of the afternoon there was no activity at the station. Occasionally someone would drop in for some small business or just to chat and collect the latest news from down the line.

Scot lay resting on a bench in the waiting room. Periodically he drifted off into sleep and dreams of adventure, yet every noise or voice registered clearly in his mind. A conversation over the advisability of planting due to a possible warm front yet to come had just ended when the distant sound of a whistle caught the boy's consciousness.

"Scot," Mr. Coates announced, "the afternoon freight is coming in."

The hinges squeaked as the man passed through the counter gate and exited onto the platform. Scot swung his feet to the floor and sat up rubbing his eyes. The clock chimed three as he left the room to watch the approaching train. Number forty-six pulled in on the main with ten cars in tow. She stopped in front of the station where the engineer climbed down to converse with the stationmaster. The conductor climbed down from the caboose with a clipboard in hand and ambled up to join them. Scot leaned against a post near the edge of the platform and watched.

The three men talked briefly. Then the conductor took charge as the crew of Number forty-six began the operation of breaking down the train and delivering the cars to their various industries. Mr. Coates walked over toward Scot as the brakeman dropped the last three cars and the caboose.

"What happens now?" Scot asked.

The engine eased forward with the remaining cars.

"They'll deliver these cars to their sidings and pull out those cars that are ready for tomorrow's run, and spot them on the freight track on the other side there." He pointed to the far track.

The train had advanced to the switch for the station track. The brakeman threw the points and the train pushed across, continuing back past the water tower to the cross over switches into the industrial sidings.

There was a rush of footsteps from the station building.

"Hi, Pa," Jarrett and Carry called in unison.

Mr. Coates turned as Carry, tall for her age and wispy thin, rushed into his arms. He lifted her into the air and hugged her. "Hi, Carry. How was hat-making today?" He kissed her and held her while she told him the day's highlights. Setting her back on her feet, he turned to his son for his report of the day.

"Jarrett, Carry, I want ya ta meet Scot Robinson." Their father briefly explained Scot's arrival as he introduced the children to one and other. "Let's go in and see your ma. Then maybe Jarrett can take Scot over to the Stewart Creek offices to see Mr. Tompkins."

"Sure, Pa," the boy agreed.

"Thanks," Scot responded.

As they turned into the hall door, Number forty-six continued to work the sidings as it broke down its consist and delivered the various cars.

*   *   *

Ten minutes later, Scot and Jarrett were on their way down the tracks toward the yards of the logging company. They walked leisurely along knowing it would be a while before the logging train returned with the evening load. Jarrett was about an inch taller than the younger boy and of slight build. Scot's complexion was somewhat darker from a lifestyle of exposure to the sun. They talked as they went, each seeking to satisfy his curiosity about the other.

"Did you always live here, Jarrett?" Scot wanted to know.

"I was born in Pine Bluff," Jarrett explained. "When I was eight, my pa was offered this job because the previous stationmaster had retired. We moved here during the fall of that year. But tell me about yourself. How's it that you're here of your own?"

The two turned off on the yard tracks and passed the water tower. Scot pointed to a locomotive parked outside the engine house with a light column of smoke drifting from its stack.

"Ain't that the one from this morning's train?"

"Yea. It's waiting here for it's evening run. Bob Leary and his crew will be taking it over to the station shortly."

They continued along the track toward the open door of the engine house.

Scot began, "Ya see, my pa's a surveyor fer the government. Ma's been sick a lot and stays mostly in a hospital in Washington, so's I travel with Pa on his jobs." They entered the wooden structure. "Hey, this is really neat!" Scot exclaimed. "But where is everyone?"

"Either on the mountain or working in the car shop," Jarrett replied.

Sun poured in through the tall forty-pane windows, casting bright patches of light across the floor boards, the tracks, and the work benches. Number Twenty-one sat outside on the track that ended inside the structure and the other, which ran through the building and out the back, was empty. Nothing was being worked on this week and the building stood quiet.

"The office is just outside the far door. We can stop and see Mr. Lawrence. He's the company paymaster. Surely, he'll know of your uncle."

"That's so!" Scot beamed.

They hurried down the track heading through the door to the platform beyond, which reached the length of the smaller office building. A group of five men left the building and headed through the engine house.

"Hi, Bob," Jarrett greeted as the man passed.

"Hey, Jarrett, who's yer friend?" he paused.

"Bob, meet Scot Robinson. He's new in town lookin' fer his uncle. Tell ya more when ya git back tonight."

"Yeh, got a train ta catch. Bye." The man and his crew moved on.

Jarrett led the way through the door.

"Afternoon, Mr. Lawrence," the boy greeted.

Milton Lawrence looked up from his desk. "Why howdy there, Jarrett. What brings ya by this afternoon?"

"I want ya ta meet Scot Robinson, Sir. He's here ta meet his uncle who works here -- we think. His name's ...what was it, Scot?"

"It's Hank Fillmore." Scot's voice was hesitant.

Disappointedly, the paymaster shook his head. "I'm sorry, boys. But I've worked payroll here for nigh onto a dozen years. Never had your uncle on the list."

Scot's voice shook as his eyes moistened with apprehension. "Are you positive sure?"

Mr. Lawrence rose from his desk and walked across to a file cabinet. He pulled the drawer near the floor and thumbed through the tabs. Pushing the drawer closed with the toe of his boot, he stood and turned to the boys.

"Scot, that drawer contains a card on every person who's worked here for the past quarter century. Yer uncle's not there. I'm sorry. Maybe he used another name. Ya kin see Mr. Tompkins when the train comes down. Tell him what ya know of yer uncle. Maybe he'll recognize him."

"Thanks, Mr. Lawrence. Come on, Jarrett. Let's wait for the train."

"Okay," his companion agreed. "I'll show ya the car shop while we're waitin."

They left by the opposite door and stepped out onto the wooden walk facing the storage tracks and car repair shop. The sounds of voices and hammering greeted the two as they entered the open doors of the bunk room and passed into the work area.

"Howdy, Jarrett," the maintenance boss greeted.

"Hi, Mr. Jeffers," the boy returned.

Steven Jeffers was supervising and assisting in the repair of the flat bed of a log car. A young workman, Daniel Hendricks, was also working on the car. A boy named Jeremy Baker was sweeping up and helping with odd jobs.

Work stopped as introductions were made. After visiting and looking around for a quarter hour, Scot and Jarrett returned to the office boardwalk to await the train. Several crates were scattered or stacked about, so it wasn't hard to find a place to sit. Scot found a long box against the wall and leaned back against the woodwork to survey his surroundings. Jarrett found a similar seat and leaned back to rest a bit.

"Scot," Jarrett spoke as he leaned back with his eyes shut, "finish tellin' how come yer here?"

The younger boy hooked his heels on the edge of the crate and wrapped his arms around his knees as he began. "Like I said, my ma's in the hospital an my pa works fer the government. We live where ever Pa works. Well, he was just assigned railroad work in the Dakota Territory, but couldn't take me cause it's too dangerous out there. My ma's brother is a wanderer of sorts. I only met him once, some years back. He's my only livin' kin I know of and so I was sent ta stay with him fer the year Pa's ta be gone. He last wrote from here sayin' he was workin' fer a loggin' outfit. So my pa wrote him 'bout my stayin' with him. But just after he wrote, he got orders ta leave. So he sent me on figurin' I'd be here after the letter and Uncle Hank would know of it." Scot stopped and rested his chin on his drawn-up knees.

Neither boy spoke.

"Golly," Jarrett said softly. "If yer uncle ain't here, you got nowhere ta go."

Quiet tears streaked Scot's cheeks. "I know," he whispered, "I know, and I'm scared."

* * *

Jarrett and Scot stood by the track in front of the office watching for the train to pull in. It had come down from the mountain about ten minutes ago and gone on to the mill to drop its log load and pick up the empties. Jarrett pointed out the trail of smoke as the train advanced through the industrial area. The shrill whistle announced the approaching train as it broke into view, crossed the roadway, and eased through the switch into the yard. Slowly the engine pulled its string of empties through the switches, past the storage tracks, and onto the track where the boys waited. The train rumbled to a halt as several men jumped down and headed for the office or car shop.

"Mr. Tompkins," Jarrett called to a short, dark-haired man climbing down from the caboose accompanied by two older boys and another man.

'Hi, Jarrett," the man greeted.

"Could I see ya a minute, Sir?" the boy called over the noise of the locomotive hissing steam at his side.

Mr. Tompkins walked over to the boys while the others with him headed for the office. He was tanned from working outdoors and of sturdy physical build. His clothes were darkened with sweat and he smelled of sawdust and perspiration.

"Mr. Tompkins, this is Scot Robinson," Jarrett made introductions. "He's lookin' fer his uncle, Hank Fillmore." He explained briefly Scot's situation and what they'd found out from Mr. Lawrence.

Scot told Mr. Tompkins what he knew of his uncle and described a man of small stature with dark hair and graying close trimmed beard.

"I'm afraid I can tell you no more than what Mr. Lawrence has already said," the logging man explained. "There's no one I can recall who matches that description. I'm sorry, Scot, but I can't think of a way to help you."

Scot had expected the worse, but it still struck him hard that he was suddenly alone in a strange place with no family and no one to turn to. "What do I do now," he begged.

"Teddy, maybe I can help," a voice interrupted from above. The three glanced up at the engineer leaning out his cab window.

"What do you suggest, Jay?" Mr. Tompkins asked.

"I'm sure Clara won't mind if the boy stays with me for a while. We can find him some work ta earn his keep. In the meantime, we can check around and try ta locate his uncle."

"Sounds reasonable," Mr. Tompkins agreed. "What do you think, Scot? Jay lives at the Railroad Hotel, which Clara Stauffer owns and operates. This would give you a place to stay and allow time to find your uncle."

The boy studied the bearded face and the kindly blue eyes of the man above him. "If yer sure I'll not be a bother to ya, I guess it's okay," he agreed.

The man put a caring hand on the younger boy's shoulder and squeezed with affectionate gentleness. "Then it's settled, Scot. I'll leave you with these two for now. But I'll get back to you in the next few days to let you know what I find out."

"Thanks, Mr. Tompkins." He turned to Jarrett who smiled with relief that Scot was finding a promise of help.

"Jeremy!" Mr. Jeffers angered voice interrupted from the direction of the car shop, "jest you wait 'til I lay my hands on you!"

"It won't be boring," Jarrett put in. "Jeremy lives with Mrs. Stauffer too, and he's always in ta somethin'."

"What did he do now?" Scot asked.

"Who knows," Jay offered. "You two can climb up here if ya want while a put the "Scott" up fer the night. Then we'll head fer supper."

"The "Scott"?" the boy wondered.

"The name of this engine. See?" Jarrett pointed to the lettering under the cab window. "It's named for Scott Stewart, the original founder of the Stewart Creek Logging Company."

Scot smiled. The train had been uncoupled as they talked, leaving the engine with its caboose to put away. The boys climbed into the cab as Jay eased back on the throttle and Number two eased forward toward the switch for the engine house.

The engineer was a husky man in his thirties. He wore denim coveralls over a light blue shirt, had a red kerchief around his sweat and soot-creased neck and a denim cap perched on his head. Another man in the cab was dressed much the same. He was introduced as Scott O'Donnell, the fireman. A third man, wearing glasses and dressed in white shirt and black tie with black coat and trousers, wore a black cap with polished visor and a brass plate engraved with the word "conductor." Jay introduced him as Dan Seegers. It took some fifteen minutes to put the locomotive away for the night. Clearing the switch to the engine house, the "Scott" backed through the empty structure to the yard beyond, stopping at the water tower to fill the tender tank. Next, it pulled up to the wood piles and everyone pitched in throwing wood to the fireman who stacked the tender full for the next day's operation. Pulling on to the lead track to the through stall of the yellow and brown engine house, Jay paused over the ash pit where Scott opened the ash pan, dropping the hot cinders and ash from the locomotive's fire box. A cloud of black soot and smoke, and the odor and heat of hot coals rolled up from beneath the engine's large drivers. It swept past the cab windows and dissipated into the late afternoon breeze. Enough steam pressure remained to pull the "Scott" and its caboose into the engine house for the night before releasing the last of the steam.

The engine stood silent for the night as the crewmen and the boys climbed down. The yard was empty except for Jeremy waiting on a crate in front of the office. He bounced up to join the engineer as the six of them headed down the drive between the side of the wooden engine house and the storage tracks toward the grade crossing at the West end of town. There they said goodbye as Jarrett turned down the track toward the station. Continuing down Railroad Avenue, the group paused at Jeffers Street where Scot O'Donnell and Dan Seegers turned off toward home. Jay, Scot, and Jeremy continued toward the Railroad Hotel at the corner of Railroad and Main.

"Jeremy," Scot asked, "why was Mr. Jeffers so angry at you?"

"I put sawdust in his coffee," the nine-year-old responded. He stated the fact as though it were a common part of the day's routine.

"Oh," Scot acknowledged. "Do you always do things like that?"

Jeremy shot the older boy a quick glance, surprised that the newcomer didn't know him any better.

"He's always into mischief," Jay explained.

"Why?"

"So people know I'm here," Jeremy said. "Besides, it's funny to see what they do."

The trio had advanced half the block toward Main Street. Along the south side of the street where they walked, stretched many businesses, shops, and a few offices. The north side was mostly industry such as the hardware and millwork companies. Most shops were closing and a number of people were on the walk or riding the street, headed home from work. Still, a few horses were hitched to the rails along the walk. In front of the sheriff's office, a black gelding stood hitched with a light buggy behind. The horse was alert to all who passed.

Doc Blevin's buggy frequently stood in front of Sheriff Young's in the early evening. The two usually shared dinner and a few games of checkers together. Jeremy was fast from practiced experience. The horse was freed from the rail and backing into the street before Jay could react from the distraction of their conversation.

"Jeremy, how many times have I told ya ta leave Doc's horse alone!" exclaimed Jay as he caught the boy's arm to prevent him from backing the buggy the rest of the way into the street.

"I'll get him," Scot called as he ducked under the rail.

"No need," Jay said with a hint of a smile. "This is so routine, Ole Jack'll walk back ta the rail and ya kin hitch the reins." He gave Jeremy a playful cuffing about the ears as he released his grip on the boy's arm.

Jeremy skipped on ahead as Scot wrapped the reins and caught up. The bank marked the corner of Main. The Railroad Hotel stood across from it, a two-story wooden structure painted green and yellow. A balcony porch stretched across the street sides of the building.

The three of them entered by a back door that led off a side porch and into the kitchen. Mrs. Stauffer greeted them, sending Jeremy off to wash up and change to clean clothes and help set the dining room for super. Jay introduced Scot and explained his predicament as he sat to a cup of coffee at the table.

Clara Stauffer, a small, attractive woman of unexpected strength wielded pots from the hot spots on the large wood range to cooler areas for keeping food warm. Large baking trays of biscuits were slipped lightly into the oven. Pouring herself a fresh cup, the woman joined the man and the boy at the table. She had dark hair, which she wore long, and dark eyes which radiated kindness and determination. Scot liked her and felt confident that he would be welcome here.

It was agreed that Scot could share Jay's room. A trundle bed would be moved in from one of the other rooms. When not in use, it slid under the larger bed, out of the way.

"I forgot my bag!" Scot remembered. "It's still at the station."

Jay put him at ease. "We'll walk over and pick it up after supper. Come on, I'll show you our residence while we wash up."

*   *   *

Jarrett stopped briefly after supper and brought Scot's bag. He also informed his friend that he could work part time at the station tomorrow. After Jarrett's departure, Jay and Scot retired to their room to unpack the boy's things. A short time later, the two went out on the balcony porch by way of a hall door. The boy leaned on the rail propping chin in hands and gazing across Railroad Avenue toward the tracks. The man sipped on a warm cup of coffee he had brought with him from the kitchen as he sat on the rail resting his back against a roof post. He continued to drink, quietly surveying the night scene below, then turned his attention to the boy in front of him.

Music from a saloon on the far side of the tracks drifted in the twilight accompanied by voices of people still wandering the streets. Stars began to wink in the eastern sky as darkness stretched across toward the last light on the western horizon. The sheriff stepped out onto the boardwalk in front of his office. It was time for the seven o'clock rounds.

"Scot." The boy turned toward the voice. "I'm down ta breakfast by five-thirty in the morning and on my way ta the yard by six. Ya can get up then if ya like or sleep in a couple hours longer. Jeremy does a five-thirty wake up fer train passengers and a seven o'clock wake-up fer regular breakfast."

"Wait, I thought you drove the "Scott"? How is it yer takin' care of the passenger train?"

The man sipped on his coffee. "I take the morning passenger run and Bob Leary and his crew do the morning logging run. We switch off at noon and Bob takes the "King" to help with any mid day switching work and takes the afternoon passenger run."

"Oh."

"If ya go with me, I go first ta fire up Number Twenty-one then take her ta the station ta make up the morning coach fer Arlee. I'll leave ya at the station ta help Mr. Coates."

"I'll go with you. But tell me somethin'." The boy stood and leaned against the corner post. "How is it that Jeremy lives here?"

Jay finished the last of his coffee and set the cup on the railing. "Jeremy's pa died in a freak hunting accident about two years back. It's told he was bit by a rattler and died in minutes. Quite strange. His ma is a really good lookin' woman and took a saloon job. She became known as a pretty fair singer and started to travel the towns along the rail line ta be rid of this place. Mrs. Stauffer was a good friend and kept Jeremy whenever she was away. Then 'bout a year and a half back, she didn't return. She's said ta have found a man in some other town."

"I guess that's why Jeremy does things like I saw."

"That's so. But tell ya one thing. He's all different fer Clara. She's like a ma ta him now, and he loves her dearly and wouldn't do a thing ta aggravate her."

"I bet she wouldn't take it if he did," Scot smiled.

"Not at all," Jay confirmed. The boy yawned. "It's been a long day," the man added. "Time fer bed."

Scot took a last look at the street below. Glancing across at the station, he saw a light from the second floor residence. The rest of the building was lost in the shadows. "Strange," he thought aloud.

"What?" the engineer asked.

"I only arrived this morning, yet it seems I've been here so long." Scot looked at the figure silhouetted against the sky in front of him. "Let's turn in."

Jay picked up his coffee cup and they moved quietly to the door.

*   *   *

The light glow of daybreak crept up behind the stark silhouettes of the distant trees slightly softened by new spring growth, crowning the ridge east of town. Dark shadows lay about the company yard cloaked in a silence accented by the chirping of birds busily beginning their day's activity and heralding the dawn. The squeak of a door, the echo of footsteps, the clattering of metal interrupted the tempo of the quiet.

Scot crossed over from the machine shop carrying an armload of scrap wood. Passing it to the man in the engine cab, he retraced his steps for another load. Scott O'Donnell had braced open the firebox door and threw the wood scrap onto the grates inside. Adding some wood chunks from the tender load, he doused it all with coal oil. The boy returned with another armful, reached up to the cab, passed the scrap to the man, and the fireman repeated the load. Scot grabbed the handrail and climbed into the cab. The fireman allowed the boy to light the fire. Scot struck a match, tossed it into the pile of oil-soaked wood, and jumped back when it burst into flame. Jay worked at greasing Number Twenty-one's drive rods and the tender's journal boxes, checking fittings and inspecting moveable parts for wear.

As the crew waited for the boiler to build up steam pressure, the boy climbed down from the cab to join in the inspection. The two paused at the piston rod and Jay instructed the boy on the proper technique, then handed him the grease bucket. Scot brushed the lubricant onto the heavy round shaft and its guide rails, then looked to the man for approval. Jay smiled.

"Right nice job, Scot." He lay an approving hand on the boy's shoulder as they rounded the front of the locomotive and inspected pipe fittings.

Scot stood aside as Jay reached up under the running board to tug at the reverse linkage, checking for tightness. "Jay, what'll I do ta find my uncle? Ya said I could start taday."

The engineer was satisfied with the linkage and paused to answer. "When yer finished helpin' Mr. Coates, ya'll have some time afore dinner ta check over ta the Wells Fargo office. Ask Mr. Harris ta go through the undelivered post and look fer the letter yer Pa sent. If it's there, collect it."

"Then what?" They started toward the engine cab.

"Mr. Tompkins will be checkin round the camp this mornin fer information. I'll see him on the later runs and see what he's found. I'll tell ya what I learn come evenin'."

A rumbling inside the engine's boiler indicated the fire was up and steam was building. The sun had crept over the tree tops and cast long shadows about the yard. Outside the building, the morning dew sparkled on the grass and rail, but evaporated in a mist from the heated boiler. The safety valve on the steam dome broke into a loud hiss.

"Steam's up," the fireman announced.

"Let's go," Jay instructed as he relieved Scot of the grease bucket and boosted him up toward the cab.

Once aboard, the engineer eased back on the throttle as the fireman gave two short blasts on the whistle. Number Twenty-one lumbered out into the daylight toward the switch, cleared past the water tower, and headed out of the yard toward the station.

*   *   *

A warm mid-morning sun cast sharp shadows along the walkways and alleyways. Several wagons rumbled about the streets carrying cargo from point to point. Carriages rattled their passengers to appointments or leisure. But mostly people walked the short distances and enjoyed the chance to gossip or browse the windows.

The Wells Fargo building was a single story wooden structure perched at the corner of Maple and Jeffers. The main office faced Jeffers and was shaded by a porch roof.

Scot paused at the Herald building, a chunky two-story structure which stood next door to and dwarfed the Fargo building. The front page of last week's issue hung fading inside the front window. Headlines announced a series of train robberies in the state with the latest being on the Pine Bluff branch of the Virginia and Truckee. The boy tucked the details into his memory to share with Jay when he next saw him. Turning from the window, he continued around the corner to the Wells Fargo office.

The door clicked closed behind him as the boy glanced about the room letting his eyes recover from the outside glare. A counter stretched across the room with a ticket window at one end, postal slots in the center, and an office area at the other end. One side of the main room was edged with benches and served as a waiting room. The other served as a holding area for parcels and small shipments to be hauled by stage or freight wagon, or to be shipped by train. The mid-morning hour was a slack time for Wells Fargo as it was for the railroad. A lone agent looked up from the office desk where he had been busy making ledger entries.

"What ya need, Boy?" the man asked.

"I come ta pick up a letter fer my uncle if'n it's here." Scot moved nearer the postal counter.

The man rose from his chair which squeaked from being relieved of his heavy bulk, and waddled along behind the counter toward the mail slots.

"What's his name?" the man inquired.

The boy responded, "Hank Fillmore, Sir." He opened and closed his hands nervously while he watched the man select letters from various slots and glance through their addresses. He found the specified addressee in the forth group.

"Here 'tis," the agent announced. He passed it to the boy.

"Thank ya, Sir," Scot spoke taking the letter in his hand. He paused a moment to make sure of the name on the envelope.

The agent waited and watched. When the boy tucked the letter into his shirt and turned to leave, the man retraced his steps toward his desk.

Once outside again, Scot sat down on the edge of the sidewalk and took out the letter. Carefully he tore open the envelope and read what his pa had written to his uncle. To the boy's surprise, there was no indication as to the exact location or nature of his father's assignment. The letter was carefully refolded, returned to its envelope, and tucked back into his shirt. Scot stood up, glanced about him to regain his bearings, then turned toward Railroad Avenue heading for the Stewart Creek yards.

*　　*　　*

The car repair shop was a wooden structure straddling the end of the siding nearest the Stewart Creek office. A bunk area occupied a side area opening off of the main work area. The work area contained a length of track capable of housing one logging car and a floor area littered with work scraps and bordered by workbenches and storage shelves.

The shop was the province of Steven Jeffers, a tall, clean-shaven, red-headed supervisor whose primary workforce was Daniel Hendricks and Jeremy. When major work needed doing, some of the crew from the mountain was sent down to help. At present, a car was in for replacement of some worn planking and hardware.

In spite of his pranks, Jeremy was a valuable helper since he knew the location of everything in the shop and enjoyed being accepted by the men.

Scot entered through the large open doorway on the track. Pausing for his eyes to adjust, he heard more than saw Jeremy rattling through tin containers on the bench in search of some bolts, and Daniel pounding the nails that would fasten a new plank onto the deck of the car. Mr. Jeffers was at the drill press boring holes into a piece of iron that was being fabricated into a side brace for the staves that held loads on the car.

Jeremy turned from the bench and spotted the older boy. "Hi, Scot," he greeted.

"Mornin," Scot returned. "Busy?"

"Not a whole lot. Jest findin' bolts." The slender nine-year-old was streaked with dirt and grease and sweat. Even his blond hair was mussed up with dirt and grease where he brushed up against the underside of the car or a shelf.

"Need any help?" Scot offered as he strolled across the dirty and littered plank floor.

Mr. Jeffers spoke as he moved to the small forge, gripped the newly bored iron with a pair of tongs, and lay it in the coals. "If ya'd like, Scot, ya kin help by gatherin' the wood scraps and throwin''em inta the wood box by the stove. Then you an Jeremy kin take off if ya like." The man checked his metal for heat before continuing. "It's not very busy round here taday. Maybe ya kin get back round three and help clean up."

"Sure," Jeremy agreed. He handed the bolts to Daniel. "Come on, Scot, I'll show ya round some."

After helping as the foreman had asked, the boys left the shop through the bunk area door with Jeremy in the lead.

"Where we goin?" Scot asked.

"On a special tour of the yards," Jeremy answered.

The younger boy led the way into the engine house. Footfalls clopped randomly across the wooden deck as Jeremy showed Scot the treasures tucked away on the many shelves, and the two explored the tops of the workbenches. Number Twenty-one stood on the pit siding. As they walked along beside the silent bulk, Scot studied its shape, its lines, the details of pipes, fittings, tender trucks, drive rods. The boy was fascinated by the quiet strength of the locomotive, still radiating warmth from its morning run and soft rumblings from its firebox and boiler as it waited quietly for its afternoon assignment.

"Isn't she beautiful," he murmured, more to himself than to anyone around him.

"Want ta see her from underneath?" Jeremy asked.

"Kin ya?" The idea surprised Scot.

"Sure," Jeremy explained. "There's steps up front down ta the pit."

It was then that Scot noticed the opening in the floor between the track rails under the engine. They hurried around front and descended to the work pit. Scot gazed in awe at the axles overhead and the belly of the boiler and the red glow in the firebox. Walking toward the end of the pit, he examined the underside of the tender as well.

"Sure is neat. I've never seen anythin' like it before," Scot exclaimed quietly.

When they emerged from the pit, Jeremy led the way into the machine shop which opened off the side of the engine house. A floor bench lay the length of the room with belt-driven lathes and presses lined along its surface. An overhead drive shaft was run from a steam-driven flywheel. The boiler stood cold at the end of the room.

"How come no one's around?" Scot asked.

Jeremy explained, "Mr. Jeffers is in charge of the maintenance shops. Work is generally done in one shop each day. When big jobs are planned here, extra help is set up. That's usually for the once a year overhauls which are normally done in the winter when the work on the mountain is thin.

"Come on outside. I want ta show ya a real neat view."

They left through the shop door and Jeremy led the way toward the engine tracks and the water tower. Lengths of rail were stacked on ties in the yard along with other materials stored there for track work. The tracks from the engine house ran from the open doors a length of about sixty yards before coming together at the switch. Standing just beyond and partly blocked from view by a broad birch tree, was the wooden water tower. Weaving through the stacks of track materials Jeremy led the way to the base of the structure.

"Follow me," he gestured as he proceeded to climb the ladder at its side.

"Up there?" Scot pointed to the roof and wrinkled his nose at the thought.

"Sure. It's not steep."

Carefully, the two climbed the rungs to the lip of the roof and scrambled onto the top surface. It felt warmed from the sun as they crawled to the center peak. Gaining a perch positioning himself in a seated position on his knees and heels, Scot glanced at the view below. It really was different, he thought.

"This is kinda neat," he voiced aloud.

"Over there," Jeremy pointed, "ya kin see the town beyond the trees."

The older boy followed the direction of the outstretched arm. He had to admit, it sure was a neat view. A distant whistle caught their attention. Jeremy shaded his eyes and searched the wooded slops of the mountain side.

"There," he pointed. "Do ya see thet smoke in the trees?"

Scot scanned the area indicated. Then he saw it. A slow moving column of black smoke puffed along in a line through the tree tops. It paused. Reversing its motion, it continued to advance in the opposite direction, bending its course toward the yard.

"Yea," Scot acknowledged. "I think it's headed this way."

Jeremy turned to his friend. "That's the first run comin off the mountain. She jest went through the switchback."

"What's a switchback?" Scot asked turning toward his friend.

"That's when you use a switch ta change direction cause there ain't enough room ta put the track straight through."

"I guess it makes sense." He continued to follow the train's progress by its smoke column.

It approached the gap in the trees where the track became visible. The train broke into view. First a flat car loaded with logs, then another, then several more, the company caboose, and finally the locomotive. Slowly the train backed along the track, passing in and out of view beneath the overhanging foliage. The echoing chuffing became audible as the cars neared the company yard. The train clattered noisily across the switch which joined the yard track to the company main, crossed the dirt and timber grade crossing, then eased around the bend toward town.

Scot shifted to a more comfortable position as his legs and feet began to tingle from the lack of circulation. Glancing toward the ground, he suddenly felt dizzy as a hollowness surged through his chest and stomach. Closing his eyes, the boy braced himself with both hands on the roof and waited for the feeling to pass.

"Ya okay?" Jeremy asked.

His friend nodded, but said nothing. He waited. His head began to clear. Yet inside a feeling of sickness remained.

"Let's git down," Scot suggested. His voice was faint.

"Okay." Jeremy shifted to his hands and knees. "Go slow. I'll follow."

Scot opened his eyes and began to back toward the edge of the roof where the ladder side rails poked above the last rung.

"Don't look down," Jeremy instructed. "Feel yer way with yer foot, then grab the ladder, one hand at a time."

Scot followed his friend's instructions and gained a careful footing on the ladder.

The "Scott's" bell announced its passage through the station area as its whistle warned of the grade crossings.

"She comin into the yard?" Scot asked as he looked up at Jeremy easing toward the ladder.

"Not yet. She's got ta drop the loaded cars at the mill and pick up the empties," the younger boy replied.

Scot began a careful descent. Jeremy followed at a safe distance. After several pauses, Scot's foot rested on the ground. A sense of relief eased the sickness from his stomach as it flooded his body with new strength and cleared his head. Scot sank to the ground leaning his back against one of the water tower's wooden supports and watched as his friend followed suit.

"I never knew heights bothered me," he confessed.

"Maybe it was the sun," Jeremy offered.

"Maybe." But Scot knew better. "How long do ya think before Jay gets back?"

Jeremy scratched a bug bite on his arm. "Usually takes a half hour by the time they change crews in the station area and go over all the news." He stood and brushed the hair back from his eyes. "Jay'll take on water first before he brings her in ta the yard. Why don't we go back ta the shop. Besides, its nearly time fer lunch."

Scot smiled. "I do feel sort a hungry." He pushed himself forward and rose to his feet.

A distant whistle drifted from the far end of town as the two boys strolled toward the car shop.

*   *   *

The afternoon sun cast dancing rays through the west windows of the tiny office building. Particles of dust played merrily in the bright shafts as Jeremy waited quietly in front of Mr. Jeffers' desk. Unconsciously he brushed the bits of grit from his bare knees, exposed through the worn fabric of his faded jeans. Grease splotched his face and jeans, adding contrast to the dirt and sweat darkened shirt and wet matted ends of hair plastered to his forehead and behind his ears.

Brushing aside a rivulet of sweat before it fell from the tip of his nose, the maintenance boss studied a repair order. Occasionally he paused to pencil in a note or check an item. After a few moments he laid it in a folder and closed it over.

"Done, Jeremy," he looked up with a tired smile. "Go tell Dan ta clean up. We'll move the car out when Jay get's in."

"Yes, sir," the boy grinned. He hurried out of the office letting the screen door bang shut behind him.

In the shop, Dan and Scot knelt beside the flat car as the workman pointed out the linkages in the brake system and explained how it worked. They looked up as Jeremy dashed in through the bunk room area.

"Mr. Jeffers says we kin clean up now. She's done." He dropped on his knees beside the other two. "What ya doin?"

"Jest showin Scot how the brakes work," Dan replied.

"Boring," the boy observed.

"Maybe if you know it all," Scot remarked. "This is all new ta me."

The Scott's whistle shrieked the Main Street crossing and its bell began its rhythmic clang as the train moved through the station area.

"She's on her way back from the mill," Dan informed. "You boys can go work the switches."

They jumped to their feet.

"Race ya!" Jeremy shouted over his shoulder as he darted out the door and down the track.

Dan rose to his feet and watched as Scot quickly overtook the smaller boy, then turned to put away the tools.

The two boys ran to the switch at the main before breaking pace and coming to a panting halt. Bending over and resting hands on knees, they breathed heavily as they caught their breath and beads of sweat dripped from hair strands, nose, and ears.

Several minutes passed before the pounding pistons and hissing steam cleared the bend and broke nosily into view. The whistle called the road crossing as Jeremy pulled against the switch lever and the points creaked open into the yard track. Scot was leaning into the lever for the through track as the locomotive rumbled slowly across the yard switch. The lever gave way to Scot's weight and the train rolled noisily onto the track in front of the office.

"Hi, Boys," Jay greeted from the cab as the train slowed to stop.

Mr. Tompkins waved from the caboose platform behind the engine.

"I'll see ya after I've finished in the office," he called to Scot.

"Okay," the boy acknowledged. He and Jeremy ran ahead to the engine as the train rattled to a stand still.

"Come on up," the engineer called.

A crewman on the flat car opened the coupling and set the car brakes as the boys scampered up the steps to the cab.

"Mr. Jeffers says the car in the shop is done," Jeremy informed the man.

"Just now we're blocking the shop track. We'll move it in the morning when we back the train back out onto the company main," he observed.

Jay pulled ahead with the caboose to prepare the engine for the night. As he backed past the office toward the engine house through track, he paused for Scot to climb down and check in with Mr. Tompkins. The engine rumbled on as the screen door clapped shut behind the boy.

Inside, Scot found the chair empty at Mr. Coates' desk and plopped himself into it to await Mr. Tompkin's convenience. As he leaned back in the chair, he felt the dampness of his shirt against his back. The breeze through the screen door felt refreshing. With his toe he pushed off from the corner of the desk and spun the chair in a slow revolution.

Mr. Tompkins sat at his desk making notations in a large cloth-bound ledger. Steven Jeffers entered the office allowing the screen door to smack shut. He walked over to the supervisor's desk.

"How did things go in the shop, Steve?" the man asked as he glanced up from his work.

"The car is finished and will be moved onto the siding in the morning."

"Robert wants us to take a look at a box car over at Graham's siding. It has a cracked flange and he wants the truck replaced before it goes out on the line." He closed the ledger and put it on the shelf. Pulling a paper from another folder he stood and walked over to the shop foreman's desk. "Here's the work order."

Mr. Jeffers attached the paper to a board and laid it on his desk. "We'll take care of it tomorrow. I'll close up the shop and be off."

"Take care," Mr. Tompkins smiled.

"See ya tomorrow, Scot," the maintenance chief waved as he stepped out the door.

"Bye," the boy waved back.

The foreman turned to the waiting boy. Crossing the floor, he sat on the corner of the desk and looked solemnly at the boy.

"Scot," he said, "I've no news for you. I've checked with all the men, and no one seems to know of anyone who matches your uncle's description."

"I guess that sort a leaves me stuck," Scot smiled sadly.

"Well, we're not completely finished yet," Mr. Tompkins added. "Come tomorrow the end of the week is when many of the men leave the mountain to be with their families or just to go to Arlee or Pine Bluff and spend their money. Those who go will see what they can learn if they get a chance, and maybe we'll learn something in a week or so. Meanwhile, you could write your ma and let her know what's happened and that you're taken care of so she won't worry."

"Guess yer right. I hadn't thought of that." Guilt at the oversight and the comfort of knowing he was secure combined to ease his worry about his uncle. "I best catch up with Jay. Thanks, Mr. Tompkins."

He pushed himself up from the chair.

"Your welcome, Scot." The man stood as the boy crossed to the door and let it slam shut behind him. He watched through the window as Scot jogged across the yard toward the car shed. Then he turned to close up the office for the night.

* * *

The puffs of dust rose lazily around their footfalls as Jay and Scot and Jeremy crossed Main Street then clopped along the hotel's wooden walkway toward the back door. A bar of lye soap and a stack of towels awaited them on the long wooden bench along the wall by the porch door.

"The pump's around back," Jay motioned to Scot. "Jeremy's first so he can help in the kitchen. Besides, I usually have to finish up the spots he misses."

A plank bench beside the pump served as a place for laying towels and clothing. The three stripped off their shirts as the older boy operated the pump handle and his friend lathered up the soap.

"Brrr!" Jeremy shivered as he ducked his head under the spout to rinse out the soap.

Jay used a wash rag and scrubbed the boy's elbows and the back of his neck. He also had to go over the creases of dirt under his chin.

As Jeremy dried off, Scot took his turn.

"Boy!" he shivered, "that water is cold!"

Jeremy picked up his shirt and flung the towel across the plank. "See ya at dinner." He turned to the porch. The screen door clapped closed behind him.

"What'd ya find out taday?" Jay asked as he lathered up the cloth and scrubbed his arms.

The boy paused in rubbing his hair and let the towel rest on his tanned shoulders. "I picked up my pa's letter. My uncle never got it." He watched the man bury his face in lather. "I read it, but it don't say where my pa is or what he's doin'."

Using an end of his towel, Scot caught some drops escaping down his forehead. "Mr. Tompkins found nothin."

"Could ya pump some water?" the man mumbled through the soap suds.

The boy worked the pump handle. "What should I do next?"

Water splashed across the man's head and shoulders. He rinsed his arms, then reached for the towel as Scot let the handle come to rest. There was no comment for a moment as the man dried his face and rubbed the water from his hair.

"Tomorrow," he began as he dried his neck and began on his arms, "is the week's end. I make an extra run ta Arlee in the evenin fer workers headed off ta wherever." Scot spread his towel over the bench and opened the towel Jeremy had dropped so it could dry. Jay dried his back as he continued. "Maybe ya could ride along. Friends keep the Railroad Hotel where I stay in Arlee. We could ask around."

"Sounds fine ta me." Scot picked up his shirt and hung it over his arm. "It might even be fun."

The man spread his towel and the wash cloth, then gathered up his shirt. "We'll work out the details after supper."

The two turned toward the porch and headed in for a fresh change of clothes before eating.

"Jay," Scot looked toward his friend. "When I went to get the letter taday, I noticed at the newspaper that there was a train robbery last week."

"I've heard about it," the man acknowledged as he reached for the door handle. "So far there's no idea on who's doin the holdups."

The door squeaked open.

"The article said something about Beaver Creek." The door clapped shut behind the boy. Their voices drifted off into the building's interior.

*　　*　　*

A cascade of falling metal crashed onto the wooden floor of the car repair shop.

"Oops," Jeremy whispered.

"Now what!" the supervisor remarked as he jumped and turned from the coupler box he was working on. "How did that parts shelf end up on the floor?"

"It come loose when I put the box of bolts on it?" the boy suggested.

"If you say so." The man returned to his project at hand. "Clean it up," he instructed, his back turned on the boy.

"Okay."

Jeremy resecured the shelf supports and replaced the shelf board, then began to return the materials to the shelf.

"What was all that noise?" Scot asked as he entered the shop by way of the bunk room.

"Another of Jeremy's accidents," Jeffers replied as he turned is attention to the older boy.

Scot walked toward Jeremy and began to hand him items from the floor to place on the shelf. "Where's Daniel?" he asked.

The man approached the two boys and stood with his hands on his hips as he watched the cleanup. "He's gone to see about getting some extra help to lift this box car so we can change out the damaged wheel." He pointed to the car sitting on the track within the shop.

The older boy paused with a box of pipe fittings in hand to face Jeffers. "Jay just got in and said it's time to take the "King" out for tonight's trip to Arlee." He handed the box to Jeremy. "Can Jeremy help?"

The man looked at his pocket watch. "I had no idea it was so late." He tucked the watch back in its pocket. "You boys go ahead. When Daniel gets back, we'll close up the shop and worry about the box car on Monday."

"Thanks."

Scot helped with the last of the shelf items and the boys left by way of the bunk room.

*   *   *

The boys met the engineer and his crew inside the engine house. Number Twenty-one was already fired up and ready to move out, smoke rising through the roof vent and steam rumbling in her belly.

"Come on up," Jay called down from the engine's cab.

The two scrambled aboard as Jay and his fireman eased the locomotive out of the shed and into the late afternoon sunlight. The switches had already been preset for the short run to the station.

"You boys have a good day?" the engineer asked.

"Yea," Scot replied, standing behind the engineer's seat holding on to the door frame. "Spent the day at the station with Mr. Coates and just went over to the shop to get Jeremy. Had to pick up from his latest accident."

"Ookay," Jay acknowledged as he held the throttle steady.

Jeremy had taken a seat on the wood in the front of the tender.

"You do seem to have a lot of accidents," the fireman commented as he reached for the bell cord to announce their arrival in the station area.

"Can't help it," the boy replied matter of factly, as he watched the engine ease toward the station.

The "King" rumbled through the switches and across the roadway as it pulled onto the track behind the station. Charles McKenzie, the brakeman, stood by to realign the switch to back behind the station to the rear of the train and couple onto the combine for the trip backwards to Day's End. Jay sounded a short blast on the whistle as he stopped the engine and shifted into reverse. As the switch points slapped into position, he sounded three short blasts and began to move behind the building. The brakeman moved with the engine to set each switch as needed until the train was assembled and ready for the evening's journey.

"Bank her down, Scott. The boys and me are headed to the hotel to get our things for the trip and leave Jeremy for his chores." He set the brakes and put the Johnson bar in neutral, then stepped down from his seat. "Let's go boys."

Jay and the boys climbed down from the locomotive and headed across the station platform toward the hotel.

* * *

Jay set the Johnson bar in reverse and eased back on the throttle as Scott pulled the bell rope to set the rhythmic ringing as the train began its reverse trip toward Day's End. The consist rumbled through the switches and onto the main, then picked up speed as it headed west.

Scot stood beside the engineer's seat with his arm resting on the edge, as he watched his friend get the train underway. Jay stepped down from his seat and turned to the boy.

"Scot, how'd you like to learn how to run this train? Climb on up here and I'll show you."

A smile lit up the boy's face as he scrambled to climb onto the seat. "Yes, Sir! You really mean it?"

"Absolutely. I taught Mr. Tompkins' son, Brett, how to run this and the Scott. He ended up saving the logging train and its crew during a forest fire last summer."

"Golleee!"

"This lever in front is the throttle. It controls the speed. Down here," he pointed to a stand in front of the seat platform, "is the brake, and beside it, this tall lever is called the Johnson bar. It sets direction – forward, reverse, stop. I'll take care of these for now."

The boy nodded as he checked out each item, then glanced in wonder at the maze of pipes and valves and gauges arrayed around the boiler.

"Give me your hand," Jay instructed as he took the boy's hand and placed it on the throttle. "Squeeze this grip." He squeezed the boy's hand releasing the throttle from its locked position. "That holds the throttle in position until you want to change speed." The two looked at each other and the boy nodded understanding. "Now you try it."

Scot released the throttle and the engineer moved his hand forward and backward ever so slightly. The boy smiled. The man let go of his hand.

"Now you release the throttle, pull it back one notch, and let it lock into position."

The boy did as instructed and the engine increased its speed slightly.

"Since we're running in reverse, you have to keep your eyes on the track ahead by hanging your head out the window and looking past the tender." He pointed out the engineer's cab window. "See the curve up ahead? It's about a quarter mile out, but we start now to slow down for it.

"I see it," the boy acknowledged.

"Now ease the throttle in one notch." Scot did as instructed. "Wait for the engine to start to slow." He paused. "Now ease in another notch." The engine slowed some more. "It's not a sharp curve, so one more notch and we're good with our speed."

Scot locked in the throttle and felt a sense of pride as the train rounded the curve.

"Now, one notch at a time, ease her back up to speed," the man continued.

Once more, the boy did as instructed and the train resumed its running speed. He rested his hand on the throttle as he watched the countryside flash past outside the cab window.

"This has to be the greatest job in the world!" Scot exclaimed.

"I think so," Jay agreed.

Scott added his opinion as well. "I sure like it. Wouldn't trade it for anything." He stepped down from his fireman's seat. "You know, this girl wouldn't run like this if you didn't feed her. You want ta give it a try?"

"Go ahead," Jay encouraged. "I'll trade places with ya."

Scot followed the fireman to the tender as the engineer reclaimed his seat.

"Grab a chunk of firewood and take it to the firebox. Kick the door open like this." He used the toe of his boot to lift the latch and swing open the firebox door. "Then toss the wood in."

Scot did as instructed while the man followed with a second chunk of wood, then closed the door.

"Good job, Scot." He resumed his seat. "Later, I'll teach you what some of these gauges and valves do."

The boy returned to his place by the engineer's seat and watched the coach cars of the train out the front door past the boiler, as the countryside on either side receded into the distance. After five minutes of quiet running, Jay began again.

"Okay, Scot. Let's start to bring her in to the station at Day's End. You can't see it yet but that hill up ahead on the right is our landmark to begin to slow down. Hop up here and slow her down, one notch at a time, until I tell you to stop. Count to five between notches."

Scot resumed his place on Jay's seat and began to slow the train. As it rounded the hill, he could see the station in the distance about a quarter mile out.

"I'll take it from here." The man traded places with the boy.

The train eased into the station area, slowing to a stop. The boy watched the activity as a few folks got off the train and others got on. Meanwhile, the brakeman, Charles McKenzie, came out onto the combine car's platform, turned down the brake handle, then climbed down and opened the coupler. He waved all clear to the engineer. Jay sounded three short blasts of the whistle, Scott started the bell to ringing, and the engine backed through preset switches onto the pass track. Charles walked over and closed the last switch and the engine moved past the train toward what would become the front of the train as it headed east toward Arlee. Riding the front pilot of the engine, Charles rode to the front of the train where he stepped down and cleared the switch for the engine to move back onto the main. Once recoupled, the train waited for the conductor to signal for departure. Dan Seegers walked up to the engine.

"No one is getting off at Snow Shoe," he called up to Jay. "We can high ball past the station and go on to Kingston."

"Thanks," Jay called back.

Dan returned to the train, called "All aboard!" then climbed the steps to the car.

Jay acknowledged with two blasts of his whistle and the train began to ease out of the station with bell ringing. Once clear, the bell stopped and the train picked up speed. He locked the throttle and stepped down.

"Okay, Scot. Climb back up here and you're gonna take her past Snow Shoe to Kingston."

The boy scrambled back quickly to the engineer's seat.

"It will be easier to see where we're going now since you can watch out the front door past the running board along the side of the boiler to see the track in front."

Together the two watched the scene ahead. The man pointed.

"See that white post up ahead on the right." The boy nodded. "There's a "W" on it that means whistle for a road crossing. Give me your hand."

He took the boy's hand and raised it to the wooden handle of the whistle cord. "Grab it." The boy did. The man pulled, released, pulled, and the whistle sounded two long blasts, a short screech, then one long trailing blast as the train shot across a dirt road grade crossing. He released the boy's hand.

"What did ya think?"

"Wow!"

"Next time I'll tell you and you can do it."

"Okay!"

Another five minutes passed.

"We're nearing Snow Shoe. We don't have to stop, but we do have to slow down for the curves in the track. So grab the throttle and slow her as I tell you."

The train slowed to the preset speed the engineer had chosen. He pointed ahead.

"There's the whistle post. Start as soon as we pass it."

The train sped past the post and Scot sounded the whistle. As he reached the last long blast, they flashed past the station and faded into the distance along with the trailing sound of the whistle.

*   *   *

The journey to Arlee continued with ongoing lessons and practice along the line between station stops, the two men sharing their love of their jobs with the wonder and joy of their student as he began to learn how to operate a steam locomotive, their locomotive, the "R L King" Number Twenty-one.

*   *   *

An hour and a half later, the train pulled into the station at Arlee. Jay left his fireman in charge to take the "King" to the engine yard, service it in preparation for Saturday's return trip, turn in on the turntable, reassemble the train, and put it to bed for the night. Jay and the boy left for the hotel across the street from the station. The train crew would settle in for the night in the bunk room above the station's freight room.

The two entered the lobby of the hotel, alive with the activity of newly arrived passengers checking in for the night. Jay held back while the lady at the front desk finished checking in the last guest. A man and his son stood by to escort guests upstairs to their rooms. A quiet settled as the last to check in followed up the stairs to find their rooms. Jay approached the woman as she looked up from the guest book.

"Evenin', Jay," she greeted. "I have your room key right here." The woman turned and retrieved a key from the room's mail slot.

"Evenin', Nancy," he replied. "I'd like you to meet a friend of mine, Scot Robinson. When you're finished here, we'll share his story with you and the family."

The boy and his pa started down the steps.

"Hi, Jay!" they greeted as soon as they saw the engineer standing in the lobby.

"Hi, Hank. Hi, Jason," he greeted in return. "Always good to see you and your family. Scot, this is Mr. Johnston and his son. He runs the Wells Fargo office here in Arlee and his wife runs the hotel."

"Honey," Nancy cut in. "This is Scot Robinson. Let's all go into the kitchen and have some supper while we learn his story."

"Hi," Scot waved sheepishly, momentarily uncomfortable with the attention.

"We'll follow," Jay stated as the group turned down the hall toward the kitchen in the back of the building.

* * *

All had settled to the kitchen table as the woman brought cups and a pot of coffee to the table and her son retrieved a pitcher of milk from the ice box. Glasses were on the table along with place settings for the evening meal. Placing the coffee on the table, Mrs. Johnston gathered another place setting for Scot.

The aroma of a roast with vegetables wafted from the oven of the wood stove range along the sidewall of the room. While the men and boys poured their coffee and milk, the woman took the roasting pan from the oven and set it on the side board counter where she put the roast on a platter, emptied the rest of the contents into a large porcelain serving bowl, and poured the drippings into a gravy dish. She then moved the meal to the center of the table, wiped her hands on her apron, and settled in her seat.

"… so Clara said he could stay with me and earn his keep with odd jobs.

Bob Coates has given him a part time job at the station as well," Jay concluded as the woman took her seat.

All bowed their heads for a moment of silent prayer.

"Smells really good, Mrs. Johnston," Scot complemented. "You hotel ladies are really great cooks." He watched as Hank sliced the roast, took some vegetables from the serving bowl as it was passed around the table, then helped himself to a slice of meat as the platter followed.

The meal began in an extended moment of silence as all began to enjoy the food. After a while, Jay began to share the boy's story. He set his fork down and observed the gathering. All continued to eat as he spoke.

"Scot arrived in Snow Shoe earlier this week, looking for his uncle. It seems the uncle was never there, so we've begun a search to find out what happened to him and the boy is staying with me until we find him."

"My pa's last letter said I was ta stay with my Uncle Hank while he got settled in his new assignment somewhere out west, and that Uncle Hank worked for the logging company. But we found out he was never there, and he never got my pa's letter, cause it was still at the Wells Fargo office." He mashed his potato and poured some drippings on it.

"Sounds quite the mystery," Nancy commented.

"Can we help?" her son spoke up.

"I'm sorry," Hank began. "This is our son, Jason."

"Hi." Jason nodded toward Scot. "I just hang around and do whatever is needed," he smiled jokingly.

"Okay, Son. I should have introduced you in the lobby when we first met," his ma apologized.

"That's okay. We know each other now," Scot rescued.

"Have any idea what happened to your uncle?" Jason asked.

"Not yet," the older boy replied. "We're not sure where to start looking for him. It doesn't seem he ever was in Snow Shoe."

There was a quiet pause as all refocused on the meal.

After a while, Jay ventured a question.

"Hank, perhaps you and me can put together a plan for a search."

"After dinner we can explore ideas and maybe come up with something," the man replied.

"Maybe we can help," Jason offered.

"I sure hope so," Scot put in. "I don't know what to do."

The meal ended with cookies Mrs. Johnston had baked earlier in the day.

"Jason," Mr. Johnston instructed, "why don't you boys tend the stove in the parlor and we'll be along after we clean up here."

"Okay, Pa."

The boys left the kitchen.

Following cleanup, all adjourned into the parlor to consider possibilities.

The Johnstons settled on the parlor sofa, the boys on the floor near the stove, and Jay in a wooden Boston rocker.

"Hank," Jay began. "You work for Wells Fargo, right."

"Yea."

"Do they have offices all along the rail line? Can you share Scot's story and see if anyone might have any information?"

"I'll send a telegram to all offices throughout the Virginia and Truckee system." He turned to Scot. "Scot, can you tell me all you know about you uncle's appearance and what he does?"

"I really don't know where he's been or what he does." The boy paused to scratch his head and think a moment. "Ma never did say what her brother did for work. I met him once. He liked to joke around and make you laugh. Just then he had a full beard, closely trimmed. He had a full head of hair, fairly thick and clean trimmed, seemed a light brown and his beard had a lot of white in it. He's not real tall, kinda average. And he's average size, not fat. He likes dark clothes with a white shirt and a coat. Not much more I can think of." He paused. "Oh yea. He wears a flat brimmed black hat."

"He could almost be anybody," Jason suggested.

"A lot of people could look like that," Jay added.

Mr. Johnston walked over to a desk beside the hall doorway, and picked up a pencil and a piece of paper. Returning to his seat, he used a side table to set the paper on and make notes from Scot's description.

Leaving the paper and pencil on the table, he turned his attention back to the boy.

"I'll get this out tomorrow and let you know if I learn anything. If I do, I'll send a telegram to Ephram in Snow Shoe."

"Thanks," Scot acknowledged.

"There's a box of dominoes in the bookcase," Nancy offered. "You boys can set up a game on the floor and we can catch up on the news with Jay."

"Thanks, Ma." He rose to his feet to retrieve the box.

The boys set up the game while the engineer addressed his friends.

"Hank, there was a story in our paper about a hold up on a train. Do you know anything about this?"

The woman stood up. "While you men visit, I'll make us a fresh pot of coffee." She left the room.

Hank slid to the end of the sofa closest to the rocking chair.

"Colton Martin is the agent at Cripple Creek, the small town north of Smithville where the train holdup took place. He reported that a lone agent entered the mail car just as the train crossed the bridge over Cripple Creek, the stream that the town got its name from. He had a gun and ordered the mail clerk to open the safe and put the contents in a flour sack he had with him."

Nancy returned to the room and sat beside her husband to hear the ongoing story.

"There's never been a train robbery before and he didn't know what else to do but do as he was told. Several branch banks were transferring funds to the main Wells Fargo Bank in Pine Bluff, so there was more than $200,000.00 in cash and bank notes. There's not much the robber can do with the bank notes, but he did get nearly $80,000.00 in cash. He knocked the clerk out with his gun, so no one knew anything till after he got away.

Once off the bridge, the train slows for the grade up to the town. The robber jumped the train on the grade where the track was straight and undergrowth was close to the track. No one saw him get away. When the train pulled into the station, a freight agent found the unconscious clerk and notified the conductor."

"Then no one has any idea as too what the robber looked like?" Jay ventured.

"Not really," Hank replied. "He wore a mask, said very little, and appeared average in every way."

"How long ago did this happen, Hank?" his wife asked.

"Early last week."

"Any news since?" inquired the engineer.

"Nope. Just now it's a dead end."

The aroma of fresh brewed coffee drifted in from the kitchen.

"Coffee's done," Nancy announced. "We'll be in the kitchen, Boys, if you want a snack before bedtime."

"Okay, Ma," her son returned. "We'll finish this game then clean up."

The adults left the room as the boys turned their attention to the game once more.

* * *

Saturday morning's return trip was a continuation of Scot's learning about operating the "King." At Blakesville, Jay instructed the boy on how to bring the train into the station, with his hands on the boy's as he worked the throttle and the brake. At Kingston, Scot worked the throttle as Jay gave instructions, and Jay worked the brake. At Day's End, Jay brought the train in and allowed Scot, with plenty of instruction, to run the engine around to the opposite end of the train for the return trip to Snow Shoe. Scot brought the train into Snow Shoe station. The final stop was a little rough, slowing appropriately, but with a slightly jerking stop at the end.

Once unloaded, the train was moved to the back of the station. The train crew left for home and the engine crew, along with Scot, turned the "King" on the wye track, took it to the engine house to service it and put it away until Sunday night. Scott Donaldson headed for home and Jay with Scot headed for the hotel. Jeremy greeted them on the front walk, broom in hand as he swept the porch. He paused, standing with broom resting against his shoulder.

"Clara's fixin' dinner. Does Scot want ta help me set the table in the dining room? We only have one guest this weekend, someone to see the bank manager, Mr. Stanton."

"Just soon's I clean up, I'll come help," Scot replied.

"See you two at dinner," Jay added. "I'd like to get a cup of coffee and set a spell on the balcony porch."

All three headed for the kitchen where the engineer got a cup of coffee, then he and Scot headed to their room. The man washed up at the wash stand and took his coffee to find a rocker on the balcony porch. The boy cleaned up, changed his clothes, then headed back to the kitchen.

"How was your trip?" Clara asked as she finished prepping a ham for the oven.

Scot took the pitcher of milk from the ice box, poured himself a glass, returned the milk, and moved to a chair at the table.

"It was great!" he exclaimed. "Jay is teaching me how to run the "King." On the trip back this morning, I ran the train most of the way." He paused to drink from his glass. "I even pulled the train into the station here at the end of the run. A bit rough, but I'll get better."

"Wow!" Jeremy whispered. "I hope I can do that when I get older."

The younger boy got himself a glass of milk and joined his older friend at the table. Clara poured herself a cup of coffee and did the same.

"We'll find your uncle, Scot. Meanwhile, Jay will treat you really special. He kinda does that." She sipped thoughtfully from her cup. "Last summer he taught Teddy's boy Brett how to run the "King" and the "Scott." Later in the summer, Brett drove the "Scott" through a forest fire and saved the train and all on board."

"I don't think I'll have much time on the "Scott" since I have jobs here and at the station. But I would like to visit the mountain one day." He finished his milk.

"I'm sure you'll get the chance," the woman assured. "I think Jay and Mr. Tompkins will see to it you get to spend a night in the logging camp."

She drained the last of her coffee. "You boys can go set the table while I work on dinner. Then get some wood in for the stoves. We've an hour before dinner will be finished."

"Sure, Clara," the boys chorused as they set their empty glasses on the drain board and left for the dining room.

The dishes and flatware were stacked on the table from breakfast cleanup.

"You set the plates where I show you and I'll put out the silverware," Jeremy instructed.

Scot set the plates as instructed and Jeremy followed and put down the flatware. The older boy followed again and put out cups and saucers, and side dishes for bread and desert, at each place setting. The younger boy followed with water glasses. The two stood back and admired their handiwork.

"We're finished here," Jeremy announced. "Now for the firewood."

He led the way out the back door from the kitchen to the wood yard. Each boy loaded up with an armful of chord wood and returned to the kitchen. I second trip supplied the wood box in the dining room. Finally, they stocked the wood box in the parlor.

Returning to the kitchen, Jeremy announced, "Done."

The parlor clock chimed the three quarter hour past noon.

Clara took the pot of boiled potatoes to the sink to drain the water and mash the potatoes. "You boys go tell Jay and the guest in room 3 that dinner will be on the table in fifteen minutes."

"Okay," Jeremy acknowledged as the two left the kitchen.

*   *   *

Jay entered the dining room as Clara and the boys set the platter and bowls of food on the table. He had with him a short, heavy-set gentleman who barely stood to the engineer's shoulders. The man wore a dark blue plaid suit with white shirt and black bow tie.

"This is Carson Easterly," Jay introduced. "He'll be meeting with Mr. Stanton this morning to figure out how to ship cash between the bank here in Snow Shoe and the central bank at Arlee. They want to be sure to increase security following the earlier train robbery at Cripple Creek."

"That's easy," Jeremy piped up. "Just hide someone behind the boxes in the baggage area and he can get the drop on the robber when he comes in." He smiled at his solution.

"Why thank you, Boy. I'll be sure to share that idea."

"You be sure Mr. Stanton knows it came from me, Jeremy Baker."

"I will, Jeremy."

The men entered the room and took seats on the side of the table beside Scot, where the engineer sat for every meal.

Clara sat at the end closest to the kitchen with Jeremy on her right and Scot on her left. "Let us bow our heads for a moment of silent prayer," she instructed. After a full minute of silence, she signaled the end with a quiet, "Amen."

"Pass the serving dishes to Mr. Easterly to start and he can pass them down the table," the woman instructed.

The dishes of food began their rounds.

"Mr. Easterly returns to Arlee on the Monday morning train," Jay stated as he placed some creamed corn on his plate. "If it's okay with Clara, and I know it is with Mr. Coates, you boys can ride along."

"Really!" the younger boy exclaimed.

"Yes," the woman agreed.

"I'll get to see the Johnstons again?" the older boy asked.

"Not this trip," the engineer explained. "We're only there long enough to turn and service the engine, then we have to leave again for the return trip." He cut into a slab of ham. Putting his utensils down, he looked up at the boy. "I'll give you a choice, you can ride the "King" with me or run over to the hotel while I'm gone."

Scot finished and swallowed a bite of ham. "That's easy. I'll stay with the "King.""

"Oh, it's the "King,"" Clara commented, "and not with Jay."

"I'll accept it's the same," Jay rescued.

"There must be something special here," the bank man observed.

"Jay's teaching me how to run his engine," Scot explained.

"Now that is special," the man acknowledged. He turned his attention to his plate of food.

A short period of silence settled on the room as all concentrated on enjoying their food. Silverware clinked on Chinaware as plates full of food emptied.

"What are you boys doing this afternoon?" Clara inquired as she started to gather the serving dishes, slide all the left overs onto one, and stack them to take to the kitchen.

"You want ta go fishing over at the Tyler farm?" Jeremy asked.

"Sounds like fun," Scot replied.

"As soon as the dishes are done, you two can take off." She picked up the pile of serving dishes and left for the kitchen.

"See you later," Jay said as he left the room with Carson.

"Okay," the boy returned as he joined Jeremy to gather the dishes and stacked them on a wooden tray from the side board, to take to the kitchen.

* * *

The room was still dark as Jay lit the candle lamp on the table beside his bed. "Wake up, Scot," he called as he rose to gather his clothes from a nearby chair.

The boy stirred and tossed off his bed covers. Sitting up to the side of the bed, he rubbed the sleep from his eyes.

"What's the Almanac say for today?" he asked as he reached for his clothes from their place on the blanket chest.

"Should be clear and sunny, so it says." He pulled on his coveralls and fastened the shoulder straps on the front, then walked to the wash stand to wash up for breakfast.

The boy tucked in his shirt as he pulled up his suspenders, then turned to make up his bed. "I guess we'll see when the sun comes up." Scot took his turn at the wash basin.

Jay threw the covers up on his bed and the two left out the door.

* * *

Jeremy and Scot passed the wood scraps they had gathered from the pile in the shop, up to the fireman who placed them in the firebox of the locomotive.

"That's enough," Donaldson reported. "You two can climb on up here and we'll get her lit."

The boys scrambled up the steps into the engine cab and positioned themselves on the footplate to the tender to await further instructions.

"Pass a half dozen pieces of firewood," Scott instructed.

The boys passed the wood from the tender load as the man carefully arranged the pieces around and over the pile of kindling scraps. When finished, he reached for the container of coal oil and soaked the wood.

"You can put this back on the tender out of the way." He passed the can to Scot who was closest.

"Jeremy," he stood to face the boy. "How'd you like to light the fire?"

"Yes, Sir." The boy dropped by the open firebox and took the offered matchbox.

He removed one match, struck it on the metal door, and dropped it on the pile of kindling. The oil took up the flame and, with a sudden swoosh, exploded into a roaring fire. The boy jumped back, dropping the matchbox. The man quickly recovered it, closed the firebox door, and stood back with the boys.

"Wow!" the younger boy exclaimed. "I never saw a fire go that fast before."

"I have," Scot spoke up. "I've lit it before. It's really something." He put a hand on Jeremy's shoulder. "I jumped, too, the first time I lit it."

"It'll be a while till it builds up steam," Donaldson informed. "You boys want to go over to the office with Jay and get a cup of coffee or something?"

"Okay," they chorused as they dropped down the steps and headed out the open bay door toward the office.

It was a short walk out the door into the predawn light, across the track to the back platform, and into the door to the office building. Closing the door behind them, the boys immediately felt the warmth of the wood stove and the crush of the men's conversation. Mr. Tompkins was busy with Steven Jeffers reviewing work orders for equipment in the car shop. Jay and the "Scott's" engineer, Bob Leary were busy coordinating train schedules for the day's freight schedule. The boys each took a cup from the hooks on the wall, walked to the stove and poured a cup of coffee, then stood to the side of the room to sip their coffee and wait for the engineer to leave for the morning run.

Five minutes more passed in this manor. Finally, Jay broke away from his conversation and turned to the boys.

"You two ready?" he asked.

"Yea," Scot replied.

The boys wiped their empty cups with their kerchiefs and hung them back up, then followed the man back to the engine house. As the three left the office building, Scot noted that the sun had dawned on the new day, bright red as it crept above the eastern horizon beyond the front of the office.

"Maybe the almanac was right," he observed.

"Just might be," the engineer returned.

"What are you talking about?" Jeremy asked.

"The weather," the other two chorused.

"Oh." His voice still sounded confused.

As the three climbed the steps into the engine's cab, the fireman announced that steam was up and she was ready to go.

"Scot, you want ta take her out?" Jay offered.

"You bet!" the boy beamed.

He stepped up onto the engineer's box and released the brake. Shifting the Johnson bar into forward, he eased back on the throttle and the locomotive began to move forward. Slowly the first loud chuffs pushed steam through the pistons as the large drivers ground noisily on the iron rail. Smoke burst from the stack and pushed its way out the roof vent as Number Twenty-one moved toward the open doors and into the early dawn. Fully serviced from the night before, the engine was ready to begin its first run of the week.

The switches had been preset for the first move to the track behind the station. Trainman Matt Kelton stood at the last switch ready to close it for the engine to move past the building and onto the station track behind the coach cars. Scot operated the locomotive under Jay's constant supervision as he passed through the switches and crept up to couple to the cars. Closing the throttle and placing the Johnson bar in neutral, he set the brake. The train waited while passengers, mail, and baggage loaded.

"Wow, you can do this!" Jeremy wondered.

"Sure can," Scot replied as he sat back on the engineer's seat and turned to face his friend.

"He's learnin' good, Jeremy," Jay remarked. "When you get older, I'll teach you, too. The railroad can always use new blood. And there's no way to learn then by doin'."

The boys turned their attention to the station activity and watched the people as they boarded the train.

"There's Mr. Easterly," Jeremy pointed as he watched the bank man board the train.

"I hope they're able the stop the train robber," Scott remarked as he checked the gauges and added more wood to the fire.

"I told him how," the younger boy boasted from his position leaning up against the engineer's seat. "Just hide someone in the baggage car to catch him when he goes in."

"Good idea," the fireman shared.

The crowd dwindled as the last people climbed aboard and the baggage wagon was drawn away from the baggage compartment of the combination car.

"All aboard!" Dan Seegers called as he waved toward the engineer.

"Okay, Scot. You can take her out," Jay instructed. He reached for the whistle cord and pulled three short blasts.

Once more, the boy released the brake, set the Johnson bar into reverse, and eased back on the throttle. The "King" came alive as the first loud chuffs pushed the drivers into motion and filled the air with noisy bursts of black smoke. The train slowly picked up speed as it headed backwards on its way to its first stop at Days End.

"I'll take it from here, Scot, until we're clear of Day's End and past Snow Shoe on our way to Chamber's Crossing." Jay traded places with the boy.

The trip to Day's End went quickly and fifteen minutes later, the train flew by Snow Shoe headed toward Arlee and points west.

"Scot," Jay instructed. "You can pull out and run from the stations. But on this trip I'll pull in, until you get more practice at coming to a smooth stop." He stood on the cab floor beside the boy. "I'll tell you when to trade off."

"Yea," the boy replied. "Folks will be happier if I don't make them loose their balance."

He watched out the cab door past the running board as the track flashed under the train. They rounded the hill and roared across Chamber's Crossing bridge. Several minutes later he traded places with the engineer and watched as the train approached Kingston. Scott started to ring the bell for the slowdown into the station. As the train pulled into the station, Jeremy climbed up onto the tender load to watch the station activity. The bell stopped. As the train paused at the station waiting for passengers, mail, and baggage to exchange the boy watched with curiosity as Mr. Easterly stepped out onto the coach's end platform and greeted another man climbing the steps. They entered the car together. Activity quieted and the boy climbed back down.

"Something wrong?" Scot asked as he noticed the puzzled look on Jeremy's face.

"I don't know," the boy responded. "Mr. Easterly just met someone getting on the train."

"It's probably another bank man meeting the banker in Kingston," Jay offered.

"Oh," the boy accepted. "Are we carrying any money on this train?" he asked.

"Monday's train always carries the bank receipts from the previous week to the central bank in Arlee," Donaldson volunteered. "Never had any problems in the past." He released the bell as the train cleared the station and Scot brought her up to running speed.

As the train approached the station at Blakesville, Jeremy asked if he could ride in the baggage room.

"It has to be real neat watching the track go away from the back of the train.," he stated. "Sure would like to watch that while we go on to Arlee."

"No harm," Jay agreed. "Would you both like to do that?" He asked as he traded places with Scot for the approach. "Anthony would probably like the company. He's the baggage clerk for the train. You can tell him I said it's okay."

"I'll let Jeremy do that," Scot responded. "I really like learnin' how to run this engine."

"All right," Jay accepted. "Go to the back platform rather than walk through the car. We'll see you again at Arlee."

The younger boy climbed down from the fireman's side of the engine and jogged back to the end of the train. He had to reach high to the railings since he was below the level of the wooden station platform, but couldn't get up from the ground. The boy walked around to the station side of the car to climb up. He knocked on the door's window glass and explained that Jay said he could ride there. Anthony Orlando saw him through the window, recognized him, and let him in.

The man looked like a giant to Jeremy as he stood taller than six feet, and was a large man used to lifting heavy packages and crates due to his job.

"Jeremy," he boomed. "This is a pleasure. I see you around the car shop and such, but this is the first time I've seen you on the train." He pulled out a crate from a pile. "Here, have a seat."

The boy sat on the crate and explained what he wanted.

"This is my first trip on the train. It must be really neat watching the track from the back of the car as it runs away from the train."

The man pulled his oak swivel chair toward the boy and sat down. "It is a very special view," he acknowledged. "But watch through the window from inside the car. Outside, you could loose your balance and fall off. That would not be a good thing."

"Thanks," Jeremy replied. "Do you have a lot to do while the train is running?"

"Not really. Sometimes there's paperwork to do and items to sort that need to get off at the next stop. But much is stacked when loaded according to destination. It's nice to have company, but you go and enjoy the view."

"Thanks." The boy stood and walked to the door to watch through the window. He glanced up and noticed a rope that ran the length of the car near the ceiling. "What's that?" the boy asked.

Anthony replied, "That signals the engineer in an emergency to stop the train."

"Oh."

Jeremy turned to watch out the window.

Anthony returned to his desk as the train continued to rock gently from side to side in its noisy advance through the countryside with the clickity clack of the wheels across rail joints. The boy watched as the wooded hillsides and close valleys with occasional farm clearings flashed by and the locomotives black smoke streamed behind the train. A mountain range approached from the distance toward the front of the train and gradually drew closer to the tracks.

"Where are we, Mr. Orlando?" Jeremy asked.

The man rose from his chair and walked to stand by the boy. "Those are Ramsey Hills coming in on the side. They will close in front and we'll pass through them at Guyer's Cut."

There was a knock on the solid wood door to the passenger compartment of the car. The clerk crossed through the room to the door.

"Who is it?" he asked.

"I've a message from Jay Miller," a man's voice responded.

Anthony turned the key and cracked the door. Before he could react, the masked man burst into the room and slammed the door shut, holding a gun to the clerk's face. The boy ducked quietly behind the stacks of crates in the back of the car to a place near the floor where he could peak through a small crack between crates.

"Lock it," he ordered.

Even with the mask, Jeremy recognized the man as the same who got on the train with the bank man. He knew there was nothing he could do without risking someone getting shot. So he stayed hidden and watched.

"Open the safe," the man ordered. "Give me the three bank bags. Hurry!"

"I can't," the clerk replied. "I don't have the combination."

"I know you do and will do as I say if you don't want to die." He cocked the gun to emphasize his point.

Anthony realized he didn't have a choice if he didn't want to risk Jeremy, and sensed that the boy was taking care to stay out of sight. He knelt by the safe and slowly turned the combination.

"Hurry it up if you know what's good for you!"

The door opened and he drew out the three bank bags. Before he could set them down, the robber struck him on the head with his gun and knocked him unconscious. Holstering the gun the man grabbed the bags and rushed through the back door and onto the platform. The train slowed for Guyer's Cut and the man jumped.

Jeremy cautiously stepped from his hiding place to make sure it was clear, then climbed on a crate and pulled the emergency brake cord. As the train screeched to a halt and he was thrown to the floor, the boy crawled to the door, unlocked it, then opened it. Dan Seegers entered from the front coach, saw the boy, and rushed to the baggage compartment.

"What happened?" he called.

"Mr. Orlando is hurt! The man robbed the train! You need to stop the bank man who got on in Snow Shoe!" Jeremy cried out hysterically.

But the man had already left the train.

Jay and Scot approached along the ground beside the train with the bank man in tow. Dan opened the baggage door. Jay explained.

"Jeremy had said there was something suspicious with the man and we caught him leaving the train." He paused to catch his breath. "What happened?"

Jeremy called down from inside the car. "The man who got on the train with Mr. Easterly robbed the train and hurt Mr. Orlando. He jumped off the back steps as the train slowed for Guyer's Cut. As soon as I could, I pulled the cord."

"Nice work, Jeremy," Jay called back. "But I'm afraid he has a head start on us and we have no way of going after him. I'll tell Hank when we get in at Arlee and he can telegraph agents all along the line. Just now, let's see to Anthony and tie this one up in the baggage room for Anthony to keep an eye on him."

Easterly was shoved unceremoniously into the baggage room where Dan and the recovering clerk tied him to the chair. The door was rolled closed. The engineer and both boys returned to the engine. The train soon got underway again to complete its run to Arlee.

*　　*　　*

"Did you see the robber?" Scot asked his friend.

"Sure did," the younger boy responded as he watched his friend start up the train. "He was the same man I saw get on the train at Kingston."

"Would you know him if you saw him again?" the engineer asked. He motioned for Scot to step down so he could take over for the rest of the trip.

"Yea. He was dressed in black with a white shirt and wore a black round brimmed hat. He wasn't very big, average height, dark eyes."

"Did he have a whitish close trimmed beard?" Scot asked as he watched the track ahead.

"Yea. How did you know?" Jeremy responded with a questioning look on his face.

"You were describing my uncle, though it could be anybody." He turned to Jay. "Do you think it's possible?"

"Let's talk to Easterly when we get to the station, before we send for the marshal." He started to slow the train. "The switch to the main line is just ahead. Matt will throw the switch after we stop and close it when we pull through."

A short time later, the train pulled through the switch, then continued the short distance to the station at Arlee. As soon as the train came to a stop, Jay turned it over to Scott and took the boys to the baggage room.

"Has he given you any trouble, Anthony?" Jay asked as they entered the door.

"Not so far," the baggage agent replied.

"Who's the guy that robbed the train?" Jay questioned as he stood before the prisoner.

"Don't know what you're talking about," Easterly replied as he looked toward the floor.

"Is his name Hank Fillmore?" the older boy asked as he watched the man for a reaction.

Easterly stared at the boy. "What would you know?" he sneered. "Called himself Horrible Hank."

"He might be my uncle," Scot stammered as he looked toward Jay. "But I sure hope not."

"Don't you know where your uncle is?" a subdued accomplice asked.

"He was supposed to meet me at Snow Shoe last week, but seems he was never there. So I don't know where he is." The boy dropped onto a nearby crate and looked forlornly toward Jay.

"I hope for your sake he's not. But I really don't know that much about him." The man became less hostile. "I'll do what I can to help you find him, but I sure hope you're wrong."

"I've sent for the marshal," Jay informed. "If you are willing to help, we'll stop down to his office after I take care of my train and report the robbery to the main office here to see what you can tell us."

"I won't be going anywhere," Easterly stated.

"Anthony," Jay instructed. "Go ahead and take care of the baggage and mail so we can move the train and service and turn the "King." Scott will take care of the train while the boys and I report to the office then the Wells Fargo office."

"If it's of any interest," the convict volunteered, "I don't think Hank has spent any of the money. He offered me a shared for scouting information for him, but hasn't paid up. I sorta think he's doing this for the excitement more than the money." He looked to the boy.

"Thanks, Mr. Easterly," Scot offered. "Maybe if that's true, he might be able to surrender, return the money, and get less time in jail."

"We'll let you know what we find," Jay added. "Thanks for the information." He turned to leave as Anthony rolled open the baggage door. "Let's go, Boys."

The three left through the empty passenger area as the conductor walked through and turned the seats for the return trip.

"Dan," Jay instructed, "you and Scott take care of the train while we go over to the office to report the robbery. We'll probably be late for the return trip."

"Will do, Jay," the conductor replied.

The man and the boys exited the car and descended to the station platform.

*　　*　　*

The first stop was the office in the Arlee station where Jay sent a telegram to Robert Coates in Snow Shoe to inform him of the robbery and that they would be late returning. He also asked that Bob Leary be informed and that his crew should continue with the Scott for the day and he would take care of the "King's" work when he returned.

Next, the three went to the railroad's headquarters offices to report to the president about what had happened and consider what course of action to take. Entering through the freight office, the engineer led the way up the steps to the main office area and headed for the president's office above the freight office. He reported first to the president's steward, Howard Roth, whose desk was just outside the president's office door. He wore a crisp white coat with a gold-plated badge with the word "steward" engraved on it

"Howdy, Howard," he greeted. "Is Mr. Marlow in his office?"

"I'll tell him you're here," the man stood toward the door.

"Let him know the train was robbed on the way in. That should get his attention."

"What!? I certainly will." He entered the office leaving the door ajar.

"Send him in!" the voice from within ordered.

Howard returned and instructed, "You may go in."

Jay and the boys entered the lavish office with mahogany wood paneling and trim on its walls and a large assortment of oak furnishings including book cases, file cabinets, desks, tables, and chairs. A gentleman in a green plaid two-piece suit sat at a desk to the far right as the three entered the office. Jay introduced the boys to a taller man, just under six feet, wearing a three-piece brown suit with bow tie and black boots under his pant legs. He stood at his desk.

"Boys, this is Mr. Philemon J. Marlow, president of the Virginia and Truckee Railroad of West Virginia." Then pointing to the boys, continued, "This is my friend Scot Robinson who's looking for his uncle, and my hotel owner's ward, Jeremy Baker." The man nodded. "We're here to report a train robbery and these boys connection to it."

"Be seated, make yourselves at home." He sat back down. "How intriguing." Turning to his secretary he ordered, "Charles, please bring my guests a sarsaparilla each."

The man left the room.

"Now, tell me what happened."

The engineer described what happened with the boys filling in the details as they saw them. Charles returned and handed each a beverage, then crossed the office to his desk, where he sat and listened with interest to the report on the robbery. Jay concluded with their concern about the outlaw's identity.

"Scot's here because he was supposed to meet his uncle in Snow Shoe. But he wasn't there and we had no idea how to find him. Information about the man Jeremy saw as the robber suggests that he might be the boy's uncle."

"What makes you think so?" the president asked, leaning back in the chair and studying the boy.

Scot set his bottle on the floor beside his chair.

"Jeremy's description matched my uncle. His name if Hank Fillmore and his accomplice said the robber used the name Horrible Hank. It may all be a coincidence, but I have no idea what my uncle has been doing or where he is. Mr. Easterly, his assistant, said he hasn't spent any of the money and might be doing this for the adventure of it." He reached for his drink.

"If that's all true," Marlow considered, "we might be able to work something out with a judge." He leaned forward in his chair and rested his elbows on his desk. "Why were you supposed to meet your uncle?"

"My pa's out west to start a new surveying job for the government and I was to stay with my uncle until he could send for me. Ma's in a hospital back East so I travel with my pa on his jobs and help out. Pa wrote to Uncle Hank, but he never got the letter. Jay's trying to help me find him." The boy drank from the bottle then set it back down on the floor.

Marlow continued. "Let's get a poster out on your uncle that you are trying to find him, but not mention the robberies. We'll put these throughout the railroad system and in the newspapers as well. You say Mr. Easterly is now trying to help?"

"Yes, Sir."

"I'll talk to Judge Nesbitt and see if we can continue to hold him in the local jail pending an investigation and later trial." He stood signaling the end of their meeting. "I'll have Charles take care of the details. You go on with your lives and I'll send word if I hear anything or need to follow up." He extended his had to his engineer.

"Thank you, Sir." The men exchanged hand shakes. "Let's go boys."

"Thanks for the drinks, Sir," Jeremy offered as he crossed the room to give his bottle to Charles.

The others offered their bottles as they left the office.

* * *

The robbery and the possible connection to Scot's uncle were the topic of conversation in the engine cab during the return trip to Snow Shoe. It dominated the evening at the hotel as all shared the experience with Clara. In the end, it was decided by all to refrain from any further mention of Uncle Hank as a suspect, and allow the search article initiated by Mr. Marlow to play out in the newspapers and the flyers seeking contact and information, to circulate and, hopefully, bring some results.

By late afternoon, the skies clouded over and a light drizzle began to fall. Heavy thunder storms rolled through by evening and overnight. Rain continued through Tuesday along with raw winds that chilled to the bone, any who were out in the storm. By late afternoon, the storm abated and the sun cut through the overcast. A bright red sunset dominated a clear blue sky.

Uneventful days followed as the boys continued their respective jobs and the routine of life in Snow Shoe carried on.

* * *

Jay's announcement at breakfast the following Wednesday changed the routine.

"How would you boys like to spend today and tonight on the mountain?" he offered.

"We can!?" Scot asked.

"You bet!" Jeremy exclaimed.

"What about our jobs?" Scot inquired.

"It's all been taken care of," Jay replied. "Bob Leary and his crew take the first train up at 7am." Between mouthfuls of breakfast and sips of coffee he explained, "Pack some warm clothes. It gets chilly on the mountain at night. Bedding is provided. I'll drop you off on the way to the engine house. Check in with Teddy. You'll ride up in the caboose."

"Okay!" the boys chorused.

The two quickly finished breakfast then hurried to their rooms to pack their carpet bags. Noisy footfalls padded back down the steps as they rushed into the kitchen to put their boots on and grab coats and caps.

"You boys have a good time. You be safe and mind your elders," Clara instructed. She stood by the table with dishes in hand to take to the drain board.

"We will," Jeremy called back as he darted down the hallway.

Jay reached his engineer's cap from its peg and followed. The front door clapped shut as the three left the building.

Upon entering the Stewart Creek yards, Jay headed toward the engine house as the boys turned toward the office. The "Scott" waited with its train, smoke drifting from its stack as steam rumbled in its belly. Bob Leary and his fireman were busy lubricating its moving parts and carrying out the morning safety inspection. The boys entered the office building.

"Morning, Boys," Mr. Tompkins greeted, standing by his desk with coffee in hand.

"Morning, Sir," the two replied.

The office was noisy with conversations as Steven Jeffers reviewed work orders with the stationmaster, Mr. Tyler handed his son a list of supplies to be loaded, and others went about their business. Brett Tompkins waited with his pa to find out what he needed to do.

Mr. Tyler turned to the boys. "Adam has a list of supplies to load onto the caboose for the kitchen at South Camp," he instructed. "Why don't you boys go with him and Brett and get them loaded."

"Sure," Scot responded.

"Follow me," Adam stated.

The four boys left for the store room to carry out their assignment. Carrying bags of flour, salt, sugar, and crates of canned goods and some of live chickens, the boys placed their burdens in the baggage room of the caboose. With all four boys, it only took two trips, then they climbed aboard the car and waited for the others to follow. They watched out the window from their seats on the table benches for the men to arrive. A short time later the group emerged from the office and headed toward the train. Two from the train crew boarded the last empty flat car to work the switches as the train moved out of the yard and up the line to the camp. The boys' fathers joined them in the caboose. Conductor, Wesley Dukeman, joined the engine crew.

Mr. Tompkins waved to the conductor as he climbed the steps. Wesley waved back. As he climbed to the engine cab, three sharp blasts from the whistle announced the movement of the train. A loud chuff forced steam into the pistons as the large driver wheels began to turn in reverse and a ball of smoke rolled upwards from the engine's stack. The train slowly eased toward the switch at the main track up the mountain and one of the crewmen dropped from the last car. Picking up speed, the train rumbled through the switch, then slowed to a short stop as it shifted into forward, and the crewman closed the switch. The "Scott" pulled its consist over the switch, gradually picking up speed. The crewman climbed back aboard the moving flat car. Settling into a slow constant pace, the train made its way up the mountain. About a mile out, it rumbled over the head end of a switch and onto a couple hundred yards of a tail track. There it stopped while the crewman jumped down, threw the switch, then climbed back on.

In the caboose, the men discussed work plans while Brett and Adam gave a running description of their travels to the two guests.

"We just went through a switch-back," Brett explained as they watched out the window at the passing landscape. "It's a way to climb a mountain when you don't have all the space you need."

"Besides," Adam added, "we have to change direction in order to get to the camp on the other side."

"Can we see out the other end of the caboose where we are going?" Jeremy asked.

"I'd like that," Scot added.

"Follow us," Brett stood and led the way through the baggage end of the caboose. "We can watch out these windows and see the track ahead."

"What about going out to the platform?" Scot asked.

"Too dangerous," Adam explained as the car rocked noisily along the track with an occasional lurch across a rail joint. "One rough bump when you don't expect it and you can be thrown from the train and get hurt pretty bad."

As if to emphasize the boy's warning, the car hit a rough connection and the youngest boy lost his footing and landed on the floor.

"I see what you mean," Jeremy barely whispered as Scot helped him back on his feet.

They watched the two trainmen ride the bumps and hold tightly to the edge of the flat car where they sat.

"Dave and Buddy are very experienced," Brett commented as he noticed the other two watching the men. "They know the danger and are very careful on how they ride."

"Sure is beautiful up here," Scot commented. "I love being with my pa in his work. He's outside all the time." He glanced toward Jeremy. "I sure can't wait to find out where he is so I can get back out with him."

"Do you have any idea where he might be?" the younger boy asked.

"Somewhere out west. But that's a really big somewhere."

The train suddenly screeched to a stop as the crewmen on the lead flat car raised a hand each and the front of the car suddenly dropped and slid to the left. The two bounced off but were able to land on their feet as each held onto the end of the car's platform. The boys rushed out onto the caboose's platform as the two men ran forward to find out what had happened. After inspecting the situation, Mr. Tompkins walked back to the engine to confer with the engineer. Adam's pa returned to the car to explain the situation to the boys.

"The track came apart and the front wheels are on the ground," he called up from the foot of the steps. "Bob's gonna see if he can pull the car back onto the track so we can reconnect the rail and move on."

"What happened?" Adam asked.

"The connector bolts had worked loose and the weight of the train popped the connector off. All the pieces are there and we just have to put it back together."

"Oh," Jeremy responded.

"You need the track tools from in here?" Brett asked.

"Pry bar and wrench should do it," Mr. Tyler replied.

Adam walked back into the caboose and slid open the freight door. Brett gathered up the tools and passed them to the man waiting below. The boys returned to the platform and the four held on as the train slowly pulled forward and the flatcar rose again onto the track. The two men walked back to join the train crew as they gathered up the loose nuts and connector plate and waited for the pry bar in order to lift the loose rail back onto the bolts protruding through the holes in the opposite connector plate. Once the rail was back in place, the nuts were screwed onto the exposed ends of the bolts and tightened down with the large track wrench.

All climbed aboard. The tools were given back to Brett who put them back in the tool locker. The train resumed the trip to South Camp.

* * *

It was mid-morning when the train finally backed onto the empty siding and dropped its string of empty flat cars. The engine coupled on to the loaded log cars, then parked while the crew took a break for coffee and conversation to explain their late arrival.

Brett introduced the boys to his friend Horace Leeds, the cook. "Mr. Leeds, I want ya to meet two good friends of mine. Scot Robinson is staying with Jay while he tries to find his uncle who's supposed to keep him until he can go on to be with his pa somewhere out west." The older man nodded. "Jeremy Baker lives with Clara Stauffer at the hotel."

"Hi, Mr. Leeds," the younger boy greeted, coffee cup in hand. "I like yer coffee and biscuits."

The cook cracked a rare smile at Jeremy's greeting.

Brett volunteered, "My job in camp is to work with Horace as his assistant. If you stay with us today, we'll teach you how they're made." He glanced toward Horace who nodded in agreement.

"You will!" the younger boy exclaimed. "Clara will sure be surprised."

Adam added, "Scot, you can work with me on Pa's crew. I'll teach you how to handle a two-man saw and spot a tree's fall."

Mr. Tompkins finished his coffee and stood from the table. "You boys run along, now. Jay'll check in on you later today and I'll take you back down on tomorrow morning's run." He left to return to the "Scott" and to leave for Snow Shoe with the loaded log cars.

"I'll help clean up," Jeremy volunteered.

"Scot, let's go get to work." Mr. Tyler stepped away from the table with his son. "First we'll find a place for your bag and get you some work gloves." The three walked toward the supply tent where the train crew was busy unloading the supplies from the train. "Tree bark can be hard on your hands."

*　　*　　*

"Horace," Brett asked, "is it okay if Jeremy works with me to make the biscuits for dinner tonight?"

The cook paused in his work checking in the new supplies and turned to face the boys. "You teach him good and I'll taste them when he's finished." He returned to his work.

"Let's get everything together before we start." Brett reached for the flat of eggs and placed them beside the large mixing bowl.

Jeremy watched.

"Bring that bag of flour," the older boy requested.

Jeremy walked over to the supply area and dragged the indicated bag toward the work table. "That's a big flour sack!" the boy exclaimed.

"It's a big batch of biscuits!" his friend replied.

The younger boy pulled the strings that held the sack closed.

"This doesn't look like the flour Clara uses?"

"It's not. It's buckwheat flour."

Brett measured flour into the mixing bowl, added salt, sugar, and baking powder, then instructed, "You stir this until it's all mixed together, then we'll add milk and eggs."

Jeremy picked up a large stirring paddle and did as he was told. Brett measured milk into another large bowl and added a dozen eggs. He stirred it into a liquid blend, then checked on the younger boy's progress.

"Looks good," he offered. "Now put a scoop at a time into my bowl and we'll mix it together."

The two worked steadily together – add, mix, add, mix, until all was blended into a firm batter mix.

"We have to fix the baking sheets next." He grabbed several metal sheets from a nearby counter and a crock of lard with a pastry brush. "Grease the pan like this." He used the brush to paint each sheet with a coating of lard, then offered the brush to Jeremy. "Here, you try."

Jeremy did as shown, but ended up with several clumps across the metal surfaces.

"You need to spread these out to make a thinner coating."

Brett took the brush and demonstrated.

"Now for flour to keep the biscuits from sticking."

He picked up a sifter, spooned some flour into it and shook it over the pan.

"This one's done. Now you try." He handed the sifter to his apprentice. "Don't let it get too thick."

Once the pans were ready, Brett showed Jeremy how to roll out the dough and use the cutter to cut the biscuits and place them on the baking sheets. Horace limped over to take a look at progress and help carry the sheets to the cook range. The biscuits were placed in the cavernous oven and chunks of wood added to the firebox. All returned to the work area and began to clean up in preparation for the next task – peeling potatoes.

*   *   *

"Like this?" Scot gripped the handle of the two-man saw.

"Good," Adam confirmed from the other end of the saw on the opposite side of the tree.

Sean Stewart, the burley axman and descendant of the company's founder, finished knocking the wedge from the front side of the trunk. "She's ready fer the two of ya ta lay her down." He stood back.

After a few pulls to get the saw teeth to bite into the bark, the two boys began to draw the saw back and forth across the cut. The start was awkward as the two tried to get into synch. Slowly they established a steady rhythm and the saw blade began to spit sawdust and cut through the tree. All around the slope, teams were busy cutting trees and the air reverberated with the hum of metal cutting through wood.

"Timberr!" the cry went out as a tree broke through and began crashing toward the ground.

"Timberr!" the cry repeated across the landscape as more trees let loose, and eventually the boys' tree broke loose and Sean cried out, "Timberr!"

The air grew quiet for a moment as crews rested to survey their progress. Then there followed the ring of axes as the axmen trimmed the branches from the mighty fallen. The saws began again as teams began to cut the trunks into twenty-foot sections for the saw mill. Horses whinnied their responses as the teamsters hitched the sections to the drag chains and began to remove them down the slope toward the waiting flat cars and their loading crews.

The boys paused after the last section cut on their tree, to watch the activity around them. Each drew his kerchief from his pocket to wipe the sweat from his face and brush the sawdust from arms and clothing.

"This sure is hard work," Scot observed as they lay their saw across the last section. "You do this every day?"

Adam stuffed his kerchief back into his pocket. "Yea. This is what we do here – cut trees. Thirsty?"

"You bet"

"Brett and Jeremy will be along with a water bucket to share with the crews. Horace'll probably bring one, too."

Sean stood his ax against the tree. "Let's take a seat and wait for the water before we continue here."

The three sat together on the nearby section to catch their breath and wait for the water. Scot studied the man beside him. He was a muscular build from years of hard work, long reddish hair with a full long beard.

"Yer pa started this company?" he asked.

"That was my Uncle Scott. He came up here nearly forty-five years ago and bought this mountain area from an early settler who owned tens of thousands of acres of mountain land. When the first settlers came out after the Indians had been driven from these mountains, they just claimed huge areas of land. When land offices were first set up, they registered their claims and the government made them legal."

Jeremy approached with a bucket of water. "Thirsty?" he asked.

"You bet!" Adam confirmed.

Conversation halted as the younger boy handed Sean the ladle and the three took turns inhaling the cool refreshment. Jeremy glanced about the work area.

"Did you do all this?"

"We sure did," Scot boasted.

"Wow. No wonder you're so thirsty." He collected the ladle to move on to the next crew. "See ya later." He was gone.

"How long did your uncle own the company?" Adam asked.

"He kept it less than five years then sold it to Brett's grandfather, who worked for him at the time." The man gazed out across the landscape, remembering back to childhood days. "I was just a kid back then when Pa joined Uncle Scott to help with the work. That was before the railroad came and it was a tent camp where the town is now. There wasn't even a saw mill at first and the logs were hauled by wagon to a railhead outside of Blakesville.

"Well, James Tompkins had a good sense of business about him and suggested to Uncle Scott that they could build a town here and maybe get the railroad to extend the line. My Uncle told him to go ahead. He spent the better part of a year seeking out potential investors including two young gentlemen with ideas of their own – Mr. Starkweather and Mr. Graham. With their interests in building a saw mill and a barrel factory, he met with then railroad president, Jake Marlow. Mr. Marlow saw a future in this country and agreed to extend the railroad, eventually to Day's End, and gain access to the area's resources. The rest, as they say, is history. My uncle realized James Tompkins had a much better sense of business and offered to sell out and try something else." The man stood and picked up his ax. "We need to finish up here and get these logs down to the flat cars."

The boys each grabbed an ax to help finish cleaning of the branches. A teamster team brought up their horses and started dragging the first of the prepared sections down to the train.

*   *   *

The day's work drew to a close as the crews came in and hung their tools up on racks on the outside walls of the bunk cars. The teamsters brought their teams in, turned them loose in the corral, put fresh grain in their feeding bins and water in their buckets, and stowed their harnesses in the tack shed. The earlier quiet in the camp gave way to the general commotion of cleaning up and gathering for supper. Brett and Jeremy were busy setting out the tables. The train had been changed over and the last load was on its way to the mill. Adam and Scot had put their tools away and washed up for supper. They joined the other two in the mess tent, found a bench out of the way, and sat to watch final preparations for the evening meal. At the kitchen range, Horace turned chicken parts in the large cast iron fry pans scattered across the hot cooking surface.

"Horace, anything we can do to help," Scot called out.

The cook paused, always surprised when a new boy showed courteous upbringing. "You boys can put the serving pans on the table as I fill them."

He turned his attention to the large pots of cut beans and potato chunks. Empting them into a collection of large serving pans, he handed them to the boys to place on the various tables. Finally, he served up the chicken pieces.

"Ring em to the table, Brett," he announced.

The boy strode over to the large metal triangle that hung at the edge of the kitchen tent, took up the metal rod that hung by a cord from a corner, and rang it around the triangle making a loud clanging noise, drawing the crews to supper.

The four boys sat together with their fathers for supper and shared the day's activities with each other.

After supper the boys worked together with cleanup chores. The men sat around telling stories and sharpening their tools. The boys joined when the last of the supper dishes had been put away.

"Hey, Scot and Jeremy," Lyle called. "Did you boys ever hear the story of Paul Bunyan?"

"Who's he?" they asked together.

"Why only the greatest lumber man who ever lived!" Sean added.

"Horace," Mr. Tyler spoke. "You know the story best. Why, as I recall, you even worked with ole Paul once."

"Yep," Horace began. His face lit up in a way Brett and Adam were used to seeing whenever he had the chance to share his tale. He commenced his telling of the story. "I met ole Paul while working in a camp out in Washington state back in the summer of forty-eight. He and Blue, that's his big ox, were passin' through and stayed ta work the summer."

The two guests were entranced by the story. Everyone else stopped what he was doing to listen again to a story they'd heard before, but never tired of. The evening drifted on lazily as the men joined together in song and story. Darkness moved in slowly as the sun settled toward the horizon. Sharpening stones and files were put away and tools hung in their places as the men drifted off to the bunk cars and their beds. Some settled on the ground in front, or under the canvas covering of the mess tent, not minding the chill April night.

Adam and Brett took Scot and Jeremy to pick up their blankets from the storage area of the supply tent and began to hunt a place to spread them.

"There are some empty bunks in our car," Tyler invited.

"You boys can sleep in the bunk car," Mr. Tompkins approved. "Bill and I have cots in the supply tent."

The four climbed the steps into the bunk car and settled into empty cots of the men who chose to sleep outside. Each laid a blanket on the mattress, folded one for a pillow and climbed in under the third.

The empty beds were bottom bunks, so each sat on the side and took off his boots and left them under the bed.

"Put your clothes under your pillow blanket and they'll be warm when you get up in the morning," Adam shared.

"Thanks," Scot acknowledged.

A light whinnying and rustlings from the corral indicated some of the horses were up and about. Quiet movement and subdued conversation hung in the air from several directions inside and outside as the men settled in their bunks and bedrolls. Twilight slipped silently into darkness as the red glow on the western horizon faded into a rich, deep blue which reached across from the east. The horses settled. The conversations from the various corners of the car and the dark silhouettes scattered about outside, drifted into soft snoring as the men settled into sleep.

*　　*　　*

A week passed. Life drifted lazily from day to day. At week's end, Jay invited the boys for the overnight run to Arlee. Mr. Johnston had invited the boys to spend the night and share Jason's room. He would enjoy the company. On the trip to Arlee, the boys rode in the engine cab and Scot continued to learn how to run the "King." As before, Jeremy spent part of the trip in the baggage room with Mr. Orlando, the clerk, enjoying the view out the back window as the track receded behind the train. At Arlee, they rode the engine as Jay and Scott took it to the engine yard to service it and turn it on the turntable for the return trip in the morning. The train was reassembled and the fire banked down for the night. Jay and the boys went to the hotel and the crew went to the bunk room over the station freight room. Jay and the boys gathered in the kitchen with the Johnston family while dinner dishes were washed and dried and stacked clean on the dining room table for the next day. Then all retired to the parlor where the adults visited and the boys shared a game of dominoes.

Someone entered the hotel lobby and knocked on the parlor doorframe. Hank Johnston rose from his chair and went to the door.

"Clarence, what brings you here?"

"I just got a wire from Harley Danielson, the agent in Pine Bluff, that a man named Hank Fillmore had stopped in with one a Mr. Marlow's flyers asking about the boy, Scot Robinson." He handed the paper to Hank. "Is there any answer?" The man leaned his back against the door frame and waited.

Mr. Johnston skimmed the message. "Yes, ask if Mr. Fillmore is still there and if so, can he take tomorrow's train to Arlee. His nephew is here at the hotel, visiting friends. I will pay his fare at this end, please notify the station master."

"I'll be right back with an answer." The man left.

"The boy's uncle?" Jay asked.

"I hope so!" Scot cried with joyful expectation.

"What time is tomorrow's train?" Jeremy asked as he paused with domino in hand. He placed it in the lineup on the floor.

"There's one northbound and one southbound around noontime on Saturdays. The Snow Shoe train leaves here around eight and no other passenger traffic goes out along the line." Mr. Johnston returned to his chair.

"Is there any way we can stay over?" Jay questioned. He drank from his coffee.

Hank answered, "I don't think so. There are usually weekend passengers on Saturday's train."

"Can I stay here with Scot?" the younger boy asked. He no longer paid any attention to the game as all three boys focused on the conversation.

Jay offered, "That might be a good idea. But, Jeremy, if you recognize Scot's uncle as the train robber, you can't say anything until he's not around." He turned his attention to the hotel man. "Hank, if he is the robber, please don't do anything. Wait 'til I take the boys back on Sunday, then, on Monday, go to Mr. Marlow and tell him what has happened. Let's give time for Scot and his uncle to figure out how to find his pa. I'll tell my train crew not to say anything until we figure out how to handle this." He finished the cup.

Clarence returned with an answer. "Harley writes that the man left before he could get an answer. He has no idea where he might have gone."

"Thanks."

The agent left.

"I guess that's not gonna work out," Jay commented. "We'll go back tomorrow as originally planned."

"More coffee?" Nancy offered.

"Please."

The woman left for the kitchen to fetch the coffee pot and bring it to a side table in the parlor. Both men refilled their cups. The boys returned to their game. The grownups sat quietly with their thoughts on what had just happened.

*   *   *

Number Twenty-one returned to Snow Shoe on its regular schedule the following morning and all left for home after the train was parked and the engine serviced and put away. Jay and the boys shared their news with Clara and their disappointment that Uncle Hank had disappeared before they could make arrangements for him to meet them in Arlee.

Monday morning dawned cold and damp and quickly developed into a day of April showers. The boys did their chores at the hotel, then pulled on rain slickers and walked to their jobs at the train station and the car shop. Scot helped Jarrett load the freight wagon and park it under the platform roof near where the baggage room door usually stopped, before the older boy left for their jobs with his sister. Jamie Rhodes passed through on his way to walk the tracks to Chamber's Crossing. He paused briefly for a cup of coffee and to try and dry off some at the stove, before continuing out in the miserable weather where the rain dripped from slicker and hat brim as he stuffed his hands in his pockets for some warmth. Scot returned to the office to tend the stove while they waited for the morning train.

Outside, the rain fell steadily with a noisy cascade of water dripping from the edges of the roofs. Otherwise, all was quiet. After several minutes, the "King's" whistle sounded in the distance.

Minutes more passed before the train came into view and pulled into the station area. It arrived in its noisy majesty with dark smoke puffing, pistons chuffing, steam rushing, bell ringing, and brakes squealing. The cars slowed to a stop with the baggage room door within a foot of the baggage wagon. Scot rushed out to greet Jay and help Anthony with the baggage. Passengers disembarked and went their way or wandered into the station to wait for items from the baggage room. Scot dragged the baggage wagon into the freight room as the baggage clerk slid the door shut on the car and the train departed for Day's End.

The boy overhead a conversation in the station.

"Are you the station master?" a man's voice asked.

Scot thought he recognized the voice, but years had passed since he last heard it and he wasn't sure.

"I understand my nephew is supposed to be here in Snow Shoe some place. Would you know of him? His name is Scot Robinson."

The boy rushed from the freight room.

"Is that you, Uncle Hank!?" he exclaimed. He stood just inside the room, staring at the old man, dressed in black, with white shirt, round brimmed hat, and graying beard, and holding onto a large carpet bag.

"Why, Boy, you sure have grown!" He hesitated, studying the boy, not sure how to react.

Scot rushed to his uncle and reached around his waist in a fervent hug which the man hesitantly returned as he dropped the carpet bag.

"I sure have missed you and had no idea what to do," his muffled voice buried in the man's coat.

"What's this all about?" the puzzled man asked as he stepped back holding the boy by the shoulders.

"We understood you were working at the logging company here and Pa wrote that he needed you to take care of me for a few weeks while he went out west somewhere to a new assignment." Scot looked his uncle in the face. "He sent you a letter to explain, but you never got it cause you were never here." He stepped back from his uncle's hold. "What's happening? Do you have any idea where Pa is?"

"I'm sorry, Scot, but I had no idea about tending you or about yer pa's whereabouts." He turned to the station master. "How long has my nephew been here and what's happened to him?"

"Let's sit by the stove where it's warmer and we'll fill you in," Mr. Coates offered.

Outside, the noise of cascading rainfall continued its steady beat as it fell from roof to roof then splashed on to the ground below.

The three gathered in chairs around the warmth of the stove.

"Scot arrived here some weeks back asking for you. When no one had any idea who you were or where you were, Jay Miller, a train engineer took him in where he lives at the hotel and has helped him get a job and try to find you. I'll let Scot fill in the details. When the train gets back from Day's End I'll tell Jay you're here and you all can take things from there." He stood to return to his desk and work on the freight train roster, but was interrupted.

As the three talked, the remaining passengers hovered, waiting for their luggage. Mr. Coates took them to the freight room to sort out their items and they went on their way. He returned to work at his desk.

"I don't understand," Uncle Hank stated.

"I guess not," Scot explained. "You never got Pa's letter so you wouldn't know what was happening."

The two talked on for several minutes as Scot shared all that had gone on in his life since he arrived at Snow Shoe. The minutes passed. A distant whistle announced the return of the train.

"Train's coming," Mr. Coates announced.

"We know," Uncle Hank stated. "We heard the whistle."

The two stood to go out on the station platform and await the train's arrival. The engine backed into view through the cascading water, falling from the edge of the roof, as the rapid chuffing and grinding iron on iron crescendoed and the train slowed as it closed on the station platform. With a squeal of brakes and a blast of steam and air, the cars glided to a rattling stop. Momentarily, the splash of cascading rain water dominated the air.

The fireman glanced out the cab window then turned to Jay. "There's someone out here with Scot," he announced. "It might be his uncle."

The engineer stepped across the cab to the window. "He meets the description. Could be," he murmured. "Can you put her away after we spot the cars on the track behind the station? The crew can go in with you to help with servicing."

"Jay!" Scot called as he noticed the man at the window. "My Uncle Hank is here!"

"Scot, I'll be down as soon as we drop the cars behind the station."

The station master had rolled the baggage wagon out to the car and exchanged what few parcels there were. He started back to the freight room as Anthony rolled the baggage door closed.

"Okay!" Dan shouted as he climbed aboard the empty coach. The "King" pushed the cars forward past the station, paused for the switch, then backed them into place on the back track. The men of the crew climbed into the cab as the engineer dropped down to the platform. The engine made its noisy departure to turn on the wye and back into the service area beside the wood pile and water tower. Jay dashed through the rainfall to the center hall of the station to meet Scot and his uncle on the front platform. He pulled off his gloves and stuffed them in a side pocket as he brushed ash and soot from his sleeves.

"Hi," he extended his hand. "You must be Uncle Hank."

The two met and exchanged hand shakes.

"And you must be the Jay Miller my nephew's been telling me about." The man in black stood with a hand on Scot's shoulder.

"Let's go over to the hotel and have breakfast," Jay invited, "and get to know each other."

"Thanks," the boy whispered.

Hank picked up his carpet bag and the three turned toward Main Street, stepped out into the falling rain, and crossed Railroad Avenue toward the hotel building.

*   *   *

"...and I never knew anything about my nephew's situation or what his pa was doing." He paused to work on his pancake, forked the syrup around and a piece into his mouth.

Clara entered from the hall with a plate of biscuits. "I made these with the flour Jeremy brought down from Horace," she announced as she set the plate and a small crock of butter on the table. "Holler if you need anything else. I'll be working on the morning dishes in the kitchen. When you all are done, Scot can clean up here and help me finish." She turned and left the room.

Scot laid his fork on the plate. "Do you have any idea where my pa is?" he asked.

The man swallowed. "I haven't heard from yer pa in more than a year." He turned his attention to a biscuit.

Jay thought aloud. "If Scot's pa thinks you to be working here at the logging company, maybe he'll reach out to you here when he's ready to send for his son."

"I guess I can stay on. I haven't anything better to do. Got no regular job." He broke open the biscuit and slathered on some butter. "I sure do appreciate you having me to breakfast like this. Been a while since I et my fill."

"We can get you a job on the mountain where you'll have a place to stay, regular meals, and some cash money," the engineer offered, finishing his breakfast and laying his utensils across his plate.

"I'd be grateful," Hank stated as he bit into the biscuit. "Wow! Never had any biscuits that tasted like this!"

"Special recipe of Horace Leeds, the camp cook. You'll get them a lot on the mountain," Scot explained.

"These are really good!" He returned his attention to Jay. "What now?" Hank asked.

"Scot has his chores here with Clara, then he'll go to his job at the station." The man rose from the table.

"I'll clear the table," the boy offered.

"I'll take your uncle to the Stewart Creek office and arrange for him to go up on the midday train."

"Clara," Hank inquired. "Do you have a place I can leave my bag? If you have a spare blanket, I can take out a change of clothes and what few things I need and roll them in the blanket. I'd like to travel light."

"You can leave your bag in the wardrobe in Scot's room." She rose from the table and went to a blanket chest in the linen closet in the hallway. Returning, she handed the man a blanket.

"Thanks."

Hank pushed back his chair, stood, and lifted his hat from its resting place on the back of the chair. He picked up the carpet bag from where he'd set it on the floor beside his chair and followed the boy to his room. The two returned a short time later, the man with blanket roll in hand.

"I'm ready."

The men left the building into the noise and wet of the falling rain, as the boy began to clear the dishes to the kitchen.

*　　*　　*

Jeremy stood by Mr. Jeffers at Mr. Coates' desk and watched as the two men developed a work order for major repairs on a box car at the hardware siding which needed replacement of its brake system. He glanced up as the engineer entered the building and did a double take when he saw Scot's uncle enter with him. The boy quickly regained his composure, remembering the promise to act normal if he ever showed up.

"Milton," Jay approached the paymaster. "This is Scot's uncle, Hank Fillmore." Introductions were made around. Hank kept his blanket roll tucked under an arm. "He needs a job and a place to stay until we hear from the boy's pa. I figure you could use an extra hand at South Camp and that would give him a bunk and regular meals."

The paymaster studied the slight build of the man in front of him and wondered if he had the strength to do the work. "You ever handle horses before?" he asked.

"I once teamstered for a freight line, if that counts," the uncle replied.

"That'll do," Milton consented. "I'll go up with you on the midday train and introduce you to the company's owner, Mr. Tompkins." He handed the man a form. "Fill this out for your pay account. You can use South Camp as your address. Use the empty desk on the other side of the stove," he pointed.

The engineer excused himself. "I have to go work the morning freight movement. I'll be back later to take the train up." As soon as Jay was out the door, Jeremy followed.

The boy caught up to the man and walked with him toward the "King" which had just finished taking on water. The rain had slowed to a drizzling mist and they both ignored it.

"Jay," he spoke quietly as he took the man's hand to slow his pace. "That's him. But he's not wearing a gun."

The man stopped and squatted by the boy. The wet mist soaked their caps and clothes as rivulets of water ran down their faces. "I guessed as much. I figure his gun is in the carpet bag and I hope it stays there. I also thought that if he gets a job on the mountain, nobody there has any idea who he is other than Scot's uncle. He'll be out of the way and we can work on a plan for what to do. I'll see Mr. Marlow when I take tomorrow's morning train in and let him know what's happening." He stood and turned toward the engine. The crew watched from the cab. "You go back to work and stay in the shop away from him until he's gone to the camp."

"Okay." The boy walked to the shop and disappeared through the bunk room door.

The man watched until Jeremy was out of sight, then started toward the locomotive. He climbed to the cab and his curious crew mates, pulled out his kerchief to dry his face, and started toward the industrial sidings.

"Is that him?" Dan asked.

"Yea," Jay answered as he pulled slowly on the throttle. "Jeremy just confirmed it. I asked Milton to see if he could get Hank a job on the mountain. There, no one knows of him except that we've finally found Scot's uncle; and he'll be out of the way while we figure out what to do." He slowed for the switch, then moved on. "I have to talk to Anthony and let him know what's up and not to say anything to anyone. No one else here has any idea about Hank's other life. The only others who know are the Johnstons in Arlee and Mr. Marlow and his staff. Hank's accomplice, Carson Easterly, is already in custody and has started to cooperate and help us find Hank."

The engineer stopped the engine at the station. "I want to see if Anthony is still here and pick up the freight roster," he explained as he climbed down from the cab and dashed through the falling moisture to the building.

Returning a short time later, the engineer climbed back up to the cab and gave the order board to his conductor. "Anthony's over at the Wells Fargo office. I'll see him later. I saw Scot and asked him to check in with Ephram to let him know his uncle has arrived and is working on the mountain and to give him any mail for him. We're hoping there will be a letter from his pa later on.

"Let's go see Ryker and his crew and finish putting the freight consist together." He shifted the Johnston bar forward and eased back on the throttle. Number Twenty-one's loud response started forward once again as the engine disappeared down the track, swallowed up in the thickening mist.

*   *   *

The weather played out by nightfall and the following day dawned with wispy clouds scattered across a brilliant blue sky. Hank was welcomed on the mountain as the boy's lost uncle and began work tending the horses then joining on the drag teams. Life in town marched on as Clara cleaned up from another morning's breakfast and the boys left for work in the car shop and the train station. The train stood by the station platform, ready for its morning run as passengers boarded and the baggage area was serviced. Quiet settled as departure time neared and the train crew prepared for departure. Dan waved the all clear and Number Twenty-one began its move, pulling the train in reverse to the first stop and Day's End. As it receded into the distance, quiet settled in the station area.

Scot dragged the baggage cart to the edge of the platform near Main Street, then sat on the wagon tongue and waited. He leaned his head back against the front end of the cart and allowed his eyes to fall shut. Sleep slipped in with dreams of a reunion with his pa and was quickly interrupted by the crunch of an approaching wagon. The boy stood up as Ephram stepped down from the Wells Fargo wagon.

"What ya got fer me taday?" The man managed his bulk from the wagon seat to the ground and waddled over to the freight wagon.

Scot met him on the opposite side. "There's not a whole lot here this morning," he replied. "I'll help you load."

Ephram took a small package to the back of his wagon and opened the doors. Scot carried a single large crate and slipped it in through the door. The man held the doors open while the boy moved several smaller crates and boxes to the wagon bed along with the mail bags.

After the last item was loaded, the agent closed the doors and returned to the driver's seat. Scot stood by the front wheel and looked up to the man.

"Ephram, my uncle showed up here this morning and will be working in South Camp. Please let me know when any mail comes for him?"

"Sure will, Boy." He reached for the reins. "If you don't pick it up, I'll bring it over when I come to deliver the outgoing bags." He slapped the lines gently and his horse began to pull away."

"Thanks," the boy acknowledged.

The man reined his horse into a turn and headed back toward the Wells Fargo office. The boy turned the baggage wagon and pulled it back to its place outside the baggage room door, then ducked inside the building.

A distant whistle announced the train's return from Day's End. The station master and the boy stepped outside the station room door to watch the train pass. Bursting past the station with whistle blowing, bell ringing, wheels rumbling, engineer waving, the flash of yellow and green quickly disappeared into the hills beyond. The roar of the passing train quickly dwindled in the distance leaving the two figures to stand in the quiet morning sunlight. They turned back into the building.

* * *

Clara and the boys brought dinner to the table in the kitchen. There were no guests. Guests were rare during the week except when some salesman came to town to meet with some local merchant or businessman. Jay entered the room from the back porch and the four gathered at the table to learn the details of his trip to Arlee. The woman started a platter of pork chops around the table as the boys helped themselves to mashed potatoes and peas then started the bowls around the table as well. Each helped himself until all had filled their plates. A gravy dish followed. Milk and coffee made the rounds. Movement stopped and attention awaited Jay's news of the day.

"Well?" the woman said.

"You waitin' on me?" Jay looked around the table at the attentive faces. No one made a move on the food. He picked up his coffee and took a sip. "Okay," he continued.

"As soon as I got in, I went over to the hotel to see the Johnstons. Hank was just leaving and walked back into the kitchen with me." He paused for more coffee. "They were surprised to learn that Scot's uncle had found his way to Snow Shoe, then remembered that Mr. Marlow's notice had included that Scot was there. I emphasized how important it was not to talk about it so I could find out how Mr. Marlow wanted to handle things and we could buy time to find out where his pa is." He stopped and looked at the food. "It's getting cold. Let's eat. I can finish after dinner."

Quiet followed and was quickly replaced by the clatter of utensils on plates as all began to consume the meal. As plates were emptied, Jeremy moved the leftovers to the side board and Clara brought an apple pie to the table.

"Anyone for pie?" she offered. All hands went up and pie was served around.

"You boys want ta tend the fire in the parlor while I clear the table?" the woman asked? "We can leave the dishes till after we hear from Jay, but I'll put the leftovers in the ice box now."

"Yes, Ma'am," Jeremy replied.

The two left for the parlor while Jay remained to help clear the table and put away leftover food. The two then poured themselves a cup of coffee each and followed. They settled on chairs while the boys settled on the floor near the stove.

Jay started on his coffee then set the cup on the table beside his chair.

"Mr. Marlow was pleased to learn that Uncle Hank had showed up. He suggested that we need to allow him to stay without anyone knowing about him as a train robber and asked that he be given any opportunity to lead us to the money. He also plans to talk to Melvin Harding, the Wells Fargo regional manager, and inform him that the robberies have been solved and he and his company are working with several individuals to get the money back. Wells Fargo needs to leave it in the hands of the V&T and Melvin will be informed of the results when they are finalized. If there is any reward money, he would appreciate its being turned over to his office as there are several individuals who are making the return of the money possible. He hopes that Easterly is right and that Hank might decide to talk about the robberies and turn the money in. If that happens he can get the judge's help to make whatever deal might lead to finding Scot's father." He turned again to his coffee.

"How are we going to do that?" Scot asked. He moved a short distance from the stove as the heat began to bother him.

Clara suggested, "We might have to enable him to visit here and have more time with you, Scot. Maybe he'll begin to talk more about himself. And maybe even feel a little guilty?" She held her coffee in her hands and took a sip.

"Jeremy and me could go back to the mountain some and work there part time?" Scot offered.

"That can be arranged," Jay confirmed. "Also, Mr. Jeffers might need an extra hand changing out the brake system on that box car. We could ask your uncle to help and Clara could put him up in one of her empty rooms."

"Good idea," the woman confirmed.

"Yea," Jeremy added. He now felt the heat and moved closer to Scot.

Jay finished his coffee and kept the cup in his hand. "I'll work it out with Teddy tomorrow morning before I leave, to bring your uncle down on the morning train to start on the brake project tomorrow afternoon. I'll suggest that would get Steven the help he needs and you two time together. Jeremy," he turned his attention to the boy. "I hope that doesn't make it hard for you since you're the only one who actually saw him rob the train that day."

The boy thought a moment, then replied, "I think I'd like to get to know Uncle Hank and forget about the train robbery for now."

The engineer fidgeted with his coffee cup as he sat back in his chair.

"More coffee?" Clara offered.

"Please."

"You boys want a glass of milk? And maybe a cookie, too?"

"Sure."

"Let's go to the kitchen," she suggested.

"Then we're agreed here?" Jay stood and the others followed.

"I think it's a really good plan," Scot agreed.

"Sounds like fun," Jeremy added.

"I agree," Clara stated as she started toward the door. "With all of you – a good plan, and fun, too."

They left the room.

*　　*　　*

Steven Jeffers, Daniel Hendricks, Uncle Hank, Scot, and Jeremy all stood outside the car shop as they watched Number Forty-six, the "Kidd," push the damaged box car into the car shop. Engineer Ryker Kimball slowed his engine to a stop just inside the doors to await final placement instructions from Jeffers. The shop crew followed their manager inside as he stepped to the side of the track where he could view the entire area.

"Daniel," he instructed. "Give each a timber from the stack against the wall to place on either side of the wheels once I have the car in place."

Each of the crew gathered a piece of lumber and stood ready on the far side of the shop track. The supervisor motioned for the engineer to ease the car into place. Once centered in the shop area he signaled the stop and the placement of the timbers as chocks to keep the car in place. Ryker's brakeman opened the coupler and signaled the locomotive to back away.

The loud clatter of the Johnson bar linkage shifted into reverse and a hissing cloud of steam pushed the drive rods as the engine chuffed backwards. The brakeman climbed onto the front pilot as the "Kidd" pulled noisily away to continue its work in the industrial area. Mr. Jeffers gathered his work force for a conference to plan out the project.

"Daniel," he instructed. "Climb up and turn down the brake handle so we can see how the linkage and the brake shoes respond. Hank, you and me will watch the linkage underneath; Scot, the front truck; Jeremy, the back."

The two men knelt beside the car where they could watch underneath and each boy knelt by his truck.

"Okay, Daniel," Steven called.

The brake shaft squealed and the rods and chains rattled under the car, but nothing moved on the trucks. Steven visually traced the components of the system to try and find what wasn't working.

"What is all this that connects to that bracket in the middle," Hank pointed.

"That's the air brake system that connects to the pipe under the floorboards and runs between the hoses at either end of the car." Jeremy pointed out the various parts from the air driven piston through the linkages.

"Is that hole supposed to be there, and all that rust?" Scot asked.

"That's definitely a problem," Jeffers confirmed. "But even so, the brake stand is supposed to close the brakes." He crawled on his back under the car and worked his way toward the truck closest to the brake stand. "This should be connected to the brake stand and lock the brakes on the wheels of this truck," he grunted. Visually tracing the connection from the foot of the brake stand he announced, "The pieces are here, but they're broken up with rust."

He crawled back out. Sitting with his back against the wheel he summarized what seemed to be needed. Much of the system seems to be heavily rust damaged. Rather than patch the obvious, we might as well replace the whole system." He stood up and walked to the stove where he poured himself a cup of coffee. The others followed suit.

"Have a seat."

Each found a chair or a crate and gathered beside the box car. It was decided that the job would begin with the removal of the entire system and the ordering of a replacement. Scot and Jeremy would dismantle the brake stand while the others would work underneath. The brake shoes and hangers were found to be sound. Chain and rods would come off first before the brake cylinder, air tank, and levers. Each began on his task.

Scot removed the brake wheel and passed it down to Jeremy, then started to dismantle the system from the top down. The men worked under the car to disconnect the chain linkage, clamp holders, and rods running from the truck frames to the central levers. Work progressed slowly. Pieces were laid out on the floor as they were removed from the car.

"Mr. Jeffers," Scot called down. "The ratchet on top looks okay. Should I leave it?"

Jeffers called back from under the car, "If it looks safe, go ahead and let it stay."

Scot found he could not remove the brake stand without lifting the ratchet gearing from around it. After removing the gearing, he laid it on the roof of the car and stepped down the end ladder to the bracket holding the stand.

"Get back, Jeremy, while I let this fall."

The boy stepped aside, but tripped over the brake wheel and fell backwards as the brake stand crashed down and bounced out of its foot pocket. It landed across the floor bench full of parts and tools.

"You all right," Scot called to Jeremy.

"Not really," the younger boy cried out in pain.

Uncle Hank climbed out from under the car as Scot dropped from the end ladder to the floor.

"Owww!" Jeremy cried hysterically. "My hand hurts!"

"Don't move," Hank instructed as he approached the boy.

"His hand looks different," Scot observed as he knelt by his friend.

The nine-year-old cried loudly in continual pain.

The man knelt across from his nephew and explained, "His wrist is broken. Don't touch it."

"Daniel," Jeffers ordered. "Get Doc Blevins."

The supervisor joined Scot and his uncle.

"Jeremy, stay down. Scot, get a blanked off the bunk."

The boys did as they were told. Scot returned with a blanket and a pillow. Mr. Jeffers put the pillow under the younger boy's head and covered him with the blanket.

"Layin' there like that you'll get cold, but you need to stay until the doc gets here and can tend yer arm."

"O...kay," Jeremy replied between sobs of pain.

"What happened?" Hank asked.

"I..tried..to..get..out..of..the..way..of..the..brake..shaft..and..tripped.. over..the..brake..wheel," Jeremy explained between sobs.

Daniel returned with the doctor. Howard Blevins had been the town doctor for generations. In his early sixties, with distinguished white hair and bushy eyebrows, he was beginning to show his age in a slowed gait with a slight limp. Black bag in hand, he knelt by the boy and examined the hand that lay somewhat out of line. He gently traced the bones in the wrist.

"Owww!"

"I know it hurts something fierce," Doc consoled. "I'll be as gentle as I can. We should splint this and keep it from moving," he commented. "But nothing appears to be broken. A very sever sprain pulling the bones out of line. It will take time to heal and require a sling and no movement."

He stood and addressed Scot. "You tell Clara what happened." The boy nodded. "I'll splint it and put it in a sling now." Doc turned to Mr. Jeffers. "He needs to go home for a day's rest. Then he can do light work using his good hand only. The left hand needs a good week or more to heal."

Kneeling once more, the doctor took splints and a bandage from his bag.

"Scot, you hold his hand open like this." He carefully lifted the arm, straightened its alignment, and opened the fingers as the younger boy screamed in pain; then placed it in Scot's hands to keep steady. With the hand thus stabilized, Doc guided the splints into place under the boys fingers and wrapped it firmly with the bandage. All watched in awe as Blevins worked. Once wrapped, the man took a folded triangular cloth from his bag, opened it and tied it into a sling, then carefully slipped it over Jeremy's head and laid his arm to rest in the fabric. He repacked his bag and stood up.

"I'll walk back to my office. Why don't you boys walk with me and get this patient home."

Jeremy continued to cry softly at the intensity of the pain.

"Thanks, Doc," Mr. Jeffers said as the three left.

"See you when we're done here," Uncle Hank called out. Turning to the supervisor he added, "What can we do here, Mr. Jeffers. We've hours yet and I don't need to go. Clara will take good care of the situation."

"Thanks, Hank. I think we can finish taking things apart and make a list of what is needed. The brake cylinder, air tank and levers appear to be sound, but the connecting pipes and linkage material need replacing. I'll take the list to Gerry Fox over at Fox's Hardware and he'll wire it to his supplier. It could come in on tomorrow's freight delivery. This is his box car." He started back under the car. "Let's finish this."

Daniel and Hank followed under the car and the three continued the removal process.

*   *   *

Clara, Doc, and the boys sat around the kitchen table, as Doc explained, "No bones appear to be broken. But it sure was badly dislocated. There's nothing I can do for the pain. I don't think laudanum would be safe for such a young patient." He paused to enjoy the coffee Clara had provided.

"Can you boys handle milk and cake?" the woman offered.

"Yea," Scot replied.

"I'll try," Jeremy added.

"Sounds good to me, too," Doc chimed in. "Goes well with coffee."

The woman left the table and walked to the cake saver on the side board to uncover the chocolate cake and bring it to the table. "Scot, plates and forks?" she asked.

"Okay." The boy gathered the service from the cabinets and placed it on the table. He then went for milk and glasses.

Clara brought the cake to the table and went to the wood range to retrieve the pot of coffee. She refilled her and Doc's coffee cups, then cut and served the cake.

"I like yer uncle, Scot," Jeremy volunteered. "He's really a nice man."

"He was the first to get to help you," the older boy confirmed. "Would you have moved if he hadn't said something?"

"It hurt too much to move." He worked on his piece of cake. "Thanks, Clara. This is really good."

As the four enjoyed their food, the boys described the accident and how Uncle Hank had taken charge and the others had helped. Doc finished and left to return to his office. After he had gone, the conversation shifted.

"I don't understand how he could be a train robber," Jeremy commented. "He's too nice a man for that."

"Remember," Scot reminded. "Mr. Easterly thought he might be doing it for the adventure and excitement."

The two finished their cake and added their empty plates on top of the one left by Doc Blevins.

"We all need to get to know him better before we pass judgment," the woman suggested. "Let's clean up now and start to set up for supper. I've a chicken to get in the oven and one of you might peel potatoes." She rose from the table to get the chicken from the ice box and ready it for the oven.

The boys cleared the table and washed the dishes, then Jeremy started to lay out the place settings while Scot prepared to peel potatoes.

*   *   *

That evening the events of the day were told again for Jay's benefit. In their room that night, Scot and the engineer discussed their evolving opinions of Uncle Hank in whispered conversation. The boy hoped to get a better feel about the man in the days ahead as they worked to complete the repairs on the box car. They agreed there was much to learn as they turned in for the night.

The parts for the brake system arrived a day later than anticipated. Scot and Jeremy used the time to clean up the work area and throw the damaged parts on the scrap pile behind the shop. Jeffers supervised a general cleanup of the shop, putting materials from past jobs away that had lain scattered about for months. In the end, the shop was the cleanest it had been all season, so much so that when Mr. Coates stopped in to check on the progress of the job, he complimented Mr. Jeffers and the whole work crew.

At week's end the finished box car was returned to the siding at the Hardware Company and put back into service. Uncle Hank said he had to leave for the weekend to look up a friend and to gather his possessions from his previous place of residence and bring them back to the hotel.

He hoped to store a trunk in the hotel's store room until they heard from Scot's pa and he decided where he would go next. Clara said she would be glad to help keep Hank's things.

The man returned on Sunday's train, bringing with him a locked travel trunk, which was placed in the store room for safe keeping. He wasn't able to find his friend. Hank returned to the mountain on Monday. On Monday's run to Arlee, Jay reported in to Mr. Marlow the events of the previous week and Hank's weekend travels. They hoped he had retrieved the money and guessed he had looked for Carson Easterly, but had no idea what had happened to him. They agreed to allow Hank all the time he needed until Scot's pa was to ask about his son, then they would have to decide how to handle the situation.

*   *   *

April drifted into May. Jeremy's wrist healed. Uncle Hank's bond with the boys grew as did his friendship with the people in their lives. He began to spend weekends at the hotel in order to share time with the boys. They'd go fishing up behind the Tyler farm, split firewood for Clara, take hikes to the mountain slope, wander the town, or work on projects according to the boys' imagination. Respect grew in South Camp for his ability to work with the horses and his hard work with the teamsters. At one point Scot realized there hadn't been any explosive reactions to Jeremy's pranks; there hadn't been any pranks. Jay took Uncle Hank and the boys for a Friday overnight in Arlee and a visit with the Johnstons. Jason was delighted to see Scot again, to meet Jeremy, and to get to know Uncle Hank. The Johnston family felt a little uncomfortable that Hank would be with the boys, but Jay assured them that if they put aside what they knew they could get to know a much different man.

First breakfast for the hotel guests had been served and those catching the train had checked out. Others staying the weekend were on their way to visit friends or carry out the business for which they had come. The family settled for their own breakfast at the kitchen table.

"You did that!" Jason exclaimed as they sat at Saturday morning breakfast and Jeremy told of some of his pranks. "Why?"

The nine-year-old finished and swallowed his piece of bacon and continued. "It was so funny watching everyone spit out their coffee. I guess they didn't like all that salt I mixed in the can of ground coffee."

"That wasn't very nice," Mr. Johnston stated as he set his coffee cup back down.

"No one got hurt," the boy reasoned. "And no one forgot I was there."

Jay washed down his egg with a sip from his coffee cup. "I can certainly say that there weren't many dull moments back then. I can also say it has been a nice change now that there haven't been any recent such pranks." He paused to work on one of Nancy's fresh donuts.

"I had no idea you were such a character," Uncle Hank put in. "It sure would have been fun to have known you back then. He turned his attention to his breakfast.

"Wish you all didn't have to go," Jason mourned.

"Oh, but they don't," his mother revealed. "Jay has arranged for them to stay over and go back with him Monday morning." She smiled as she worked on a piece of bacon.

"Really!?" Jason exclaimed.

"Really," Scot confirmed. "Thought it might make a nice surprise."

"Wow!" the boy exhaled. "We can spend the day in the train yards," he offered.

"After your chores," his father reminded.

"We'll help," Scot offered.

"What can I do?" the uncle asked.

"You can split some firewood while we carry it in," Jason offered.

"Not a problem," the man responded.

There was a period of quiet while all finished their breakfast meal.

"You and the boys can go over to the station with Jay and watch the activity until his train leaves," Nancy explained. "The cleanup will be here when you get back."

"Thanks, Ma," Jason acknowledged as he got up from the table and put on his cap and boots.

Jay followed along with Uncle Hank and the other two boys.

"I'll be off to the Wells Fargo office for the morning," Mr. Johnston informed. "See you all at dinner." He finished his coffee, put on his boots and hat, and left out the hallway to the front door.

Mrs. Johnston remained in the quiet kitchen to enjoy a lingering and peaceful second cup of coffee, as Jay and company crossed the street to the station platform.

"I have to go finish preparations for departure back to Snow Shoe," Jay informed. "You all can stay with Jason until I leave." He crossed to the "King" and started up the steps. From the cab he hollered back, "See you all Monday morning. Have a good time." He crossed within to the engineer's seat and turned his attention to Scott and the preparations for the train's departure.

Moments later Jay pulled out on the return to Snow Shoe, leaving the three boys and the uncle standing in the quiet of the empty station.

"Time for chores," Jason stated flatly.

The four crossed the platform to return to the hotel.

* * *

Immediately following the completion of morning chores, the four grabbed caps and hats, stuffed feet into boots, and left for the train yard behind the hotel. Jason led the way to the tracks where "Lauer" Number Forty-three was busy shifting freight cars. They paused to watch.

"That's Abner Matthewson in the cab," Jason pointed. "His crew is putting together the Sunday night freight to go north to Pine Bluff. Tom Jennings and Number Twenty-eight are down at the far end sorting the cars for the Monday run to Snow Shoe."

The audience of man and boys found a seat on a pile of wooden ties and settled to watch the activity. For nearly thirty minutes they watched as the engines and their crews switched tracks and moved an assortment of cars in order to create the consists on their car lists.

Jeremy began to fidget and get restless. He climbed down from the pile of rail ties and watched from the end of the pile, leaning against the wood.

"You ready to move on?" Uncle Hank asked.

"We can go over to the engine yard," Jason offered as he climbed down.

"Can we ride in one?" the younger boy asked, standing to face their tour guide.

"Not here," Jason answered. "We can explore the buildings and some of the equipment and wander the yard areas." He pointed across the main line track to the back of a large rounded wooden building with high multi-paned windows. "That's the engine house. The engine service yard is on the other side." He stepped toward the track. "Follow me."

The remaining folks climbed down from the pile of ties to join Jeremy and follow Jason to the engine yards. They walked the track around the right end of the building and arrived at the yard office off at its side. The building had a store room at the end nearest the round house and an office area at the opposite end. They climbed up onto the wooden deck and entered the office.

A husky clean-shaven man stood at a file cabinet with a folder in one hand as the other fingered through the file tabs. He found his space, dropped the folder in, pushed the drawer closed, and turned to the group entering his office.

"Mornin', Jason," he greeted. "Good to see you, as always." The man walked to his desk.

"Mr. Cody, I'd like you to meet friends of mine down from Snow Shoe. This is Jeremy Baker, Scot Robinson, and his uncle Hank Fillmore." The man stepped forward to exchange handshakes. "Jonas Cody is the office manager for Mr. Marlow."

"Find a seat, everyone," he settled into his desk swivel oak chair. "There's coffee on the stove and cups on the wall hooks. Help yerselves."

"Where is everyone?" Scot asked.

"Engineers and their crews work out of here," Jonas explained. "They're all working their assignments with their engines. Office staff don't work Saturdays. It's just me at present."

Without sitting, Jason stated, "We're just wanderin' and lookin'." He crossed the room to the door out to the engine turn table.

The wooden platform outside the office bordered on a siding occupied by a locomotive which sat silent and stone cold with nobody in attendance. Beyond that, on an open track off the turntable, sat "Dalton" Number fifteen with its huge wedge snow plow on the front.

"That's the snow plow," Jason pointed out. "It gets a lot of work during the winters around here." He turned toward the roundhouse. "We'll go in this end and walk through."

He led his friends through the first open bay and past the silent engine to the floor along the back wall of the building. The first three tracks were occupied by locomotives that appeared to have set a long time.

"These engines don't look so good," Jeremy observed. He stood at the front of the first and surveyed all three.

Jason studied the three a short time. "They've been retired for several years now. But if they're needed, they're ready to go. Each has some coal and water just in case."

The party walked the length of the back wall to the opposite end of the building. A couple of engines stood in their stalls quiet yet fully serviced. Most of the tracks were empty. Uncle Hank and the boys left by the side door into the outdoor storage area. Each of the four tracks was occupied. Parts and debris were scattered between the tracks. A locomotive stood on each of the first two tracks with a steam bucket car on one and a forge car on the other. Crossing the area, the four entered a side door into the shops. They paused inside to get adjusted to the dim light and the loud noises.

Jason pointed out the different areas. "We're standing in the machine shop. That steam engine by the side wall drives the overhead shaft and each machine has a belt that connects to the shaft. Notice a clutch on each pulley that can release it from the drive shaft and stop it from turning. See, the lathe isn't being used just now. It can turn metal parts as well as wood."

The boy's voice was nearly drowned out by the noise of the machinery and work in progress around them. A stripped down locomotive sat on the second track in, above its inspection and work pit. The cab had been removed except for its front wall and piping lay on the running board in front of the engineer's side where a new air compressor had been mounted. Work crews were machining parts in the shop while others were working on the engine itself.

As the group passed from the machine shop into the work area, Jason continued. "The tender here on the first track still needs to be lettered while its engine is being serviced. The far track is a car repair track and the crews are rebuilding a coach car damaged in a wreck."

Hank and the boys worked their tour around the outer edges of the shops area in order to see the activity, yet stay out of the way. At the car shop area they left out the large bay doors, stepping from the loud organized chaos into the quiet outside.

The outside yards had several storage tracks for equipment other than engines, as well as a residence.

"Who lives in that house?" Scot asked.

The group stood on the track outside the shop and surveyed the area before moving on.

"That's Mr. Marlow's house," Jason answered. "He'll stay there some days when he wants to be in the middle of things and enjoy being surrounded by his railroad. He also has his main house on a large property on the outer edge of town where his family lives. They're very private people and I've never seen them except at church some Sundays." He started across the tracks. "The railroad stores some passenger equipment in this yard and the crane car with its service tender." He pointed to a large structure beyond the tracks. "That's the coal dock. We're on the back side, but you can see two coal cars sitting on top under the roof. The access track goes back across that bridge, circles across the yard track at the end, and descends that ramp track back to the switch at the main yard track on the other side of the shops."

"This is quite a crane," Hank observed as they approached the giant piece of equipment. "I saw one of these years ago working a train wreck lifting broken car pieces onto flat cars to carry away." He turned his attention to the boy. "Always wondered what they did with the wrecks."

Jason offered, "I'm really not sure. Sometimes they bring stuff back here and strip off what might be usable and throw it over there on that parts pile. Sometimes a car might be able to be repaired like that coach in there. But as you can see, most of what's left out on the pile is never used again."

They turned away from the crane to a track with two coach cars.

"These don't look like the cars on the train from Snow Shoe or any that I've see at the station," Jeremy observed. "They're a different color and fancier, too."

The group wandered over to the first of the pair of brown colored cars with gold trim work and individual names, sitting together on the siding.

"The "Walton" is a parlor car. At the front end here without as many windows, is a kitchen area. In the middle of the car are tables for eating. At the back is the parlor sitting area with cushioned individual chairs and side benches." He moved to the next car. "The "Lage" is Mr. Marlow's private car. It has an office area in the back which is also like a parlor, his bedroom next, a dining area, and a kitchen. He can live here when he goes out places on the railroad on his private train."

"Wow," Jeremy whispered.

"That is some classy traveling wagon," Uncle Hank added.

"I'd sure like to see inside before I leave to join my Pa," Scot wished.

The four wandered back toward a freight house at the end of the last side track. "We can cross under this bridge to the other side of the coal dock," Jason invited.

Wandering back along the service tracks on the front side of the coal dock, Scot and his uncle and young friend wondered at the size of it. After the first mass of wooden structural support, there was an open coal drop with a crane-held bucket for loading wagons. Follow that the four bay coal bunkers were topped off with the tracks for incoming coal cars and an overhead roof. "Miller" Number three stood there quietly waiting for its crew to return. Ahead stood the water tower, the "Miller's" next stop.

The four headed down the tracks toward the roundhouse where they passed the opposite end of the structure on their way back to the hotel and lunch.

*   *   *

Saturday was a half day in the railroad shops and yards. Other than Jay's return trip to Snow Shoe, there was one passenger run at midday on Saturdays. Jason and friends paused at the station to watch the passing of trains northbound and southbound, then continued on to the hotel for the noontime meal and chores. The afternoon began with a walking tour along the tracks to see where the station was with the added note about the bunk room above the freight room, and where the central freight house was with its corporate offices on the second floor and the president's office on the end with its bay windows. A smaller freight house for local businesses stood beyond the other two, and the water tower was at the end of the lineup of buildings. The remainder of the afternoon was spent in the parlor. Uncle Hank and the boys shared in a game of dominoes using a double set to serve all four, parked on the floor near the stove. Hank and Nancy settled in with the books each was reading. All went to church Sunday morning, stayed for the church dinner and afternoon social, had supper at home, and settled in the parlor for the evening.

"Hank," Nancy addressed Scot's uncle. "We've enjoyed getting to know you this weekend. Have you any news yet from Scot's pa?" She laid her book in her lap.

Hank looked up from the game as the boys paused to listen. "I've heard nothing new since I've been here." He absentmindedly gazed at the domino in his hand, then continued. "Scot has the only letter his pa ever sent about asking me to take care of him for a while." He placed the domino in the lineup on the floor. "We really thought we'd have heard something by now. Ephram keeps watching the mail and will let us know as soon as a letter comes in."

"What will you do next?" Hank asked.

"I've been working on the mountain during the week and spending the weekends with Scot and Jeremy with Clara and Jay. We go fishing and take walks, sometime up the mountain with Adam and Brett. Once we hear from Scot's pa, I'll be taking him west to wherever he's at."

"Will you be back?" Jeremy wondered.

As the conversation continued, the boys each placed their domino pieces in the lineup on the floor, then, without thinking, picked up another.

"I don't really know." Hank glanced at the game and picked up a piece as well. "I recently lost track of the only friend I've known for a long time, yet with the new friendships these recent weeks, might consider keeping my job on the mountain. There're new friends there, too." He played the domino piece.

"I jest can't figure…," Jeremy began.

"Jeremy!" Scot interrupted.

"Okay, but I can't."

"Figure what?" the man asked.

"Never mind. Let's get on with the game."

A quiet settled as the boys placed the domino pieces each had picked up and the game continued. The Johnstons returned to their reading.

The front door banged shut as guests returned and climbed the steps to their rooms. The parlor clock chimed the quarter hour past eight.

"Time to clean up boys," the woman stated. "We can retire to the kitchen for a late snack, then it's off to bed. You need to rise early tomorrow if you want to go over to the station early to watch all the activity before your train leaves for Snow Shoe."

"Okay, Ma. Just ten pieces left to play out."

The game ended and the two boxes of dominoes were packed and put away. Books were closed and set aside.

"Check the stove, Son," his pa spoke as he set aside his book.

The boy set the boxes of dominoes on their shelf and took the poker to open the stove door and check the fire. He spread the coals and added two chunks of firewood, closed the door, and turned down the dampers.

All left the room toward the kitchen.

*   *   *

Upon their return to the hotel, Hank changed into his work clothes, prepared a blanket roll, and left on the midday train for the mountain. The daily routine settled in and the days drifted by. Wednesday dawned raw and wet. Thunder showers passed through the late afternoon. The skies cleared by sundown, followed by a starlit night and a crescent moon. Friday dawned in bright sunshine, rising through the 50s during the day. As late afternoon approached, Scot wandered over to the car shop to wait with Jeremy for the train to come down off the mountain. It had become habit to meet the train and Uncle Hank, then ride the engine cab with Jay as they helped to service the "Scott" and put her away for the weekend. The four would then walk home to the hotel together.

The boys waited on the front platform of the office building, each perched on a random crate, leaning back against the front wall of the building. Time passed and the train seemed later than usual. The Scott's whistle announced its approach. The boys dashed to the yard switch on the main and watched up the valley to follow the smoke through the trees until it came into view after the last curve in the track. Backing toward them, it slowed for the switch and Jeremy called to the crewmen on the flat car.

"We've got it." He turned to Scot and showed him how to throw the switch once the train had crossed.

The "Scott" slowed to a stop and the boys threw the switch. The train then pulled forward into the yard.

Mr. Tompkins called from the caboose, "Someone go get Doc Blevins! We had an accident on the way down!"

"We're going!" Scot called as the two boys ran for the doctor.

"I wonder what happened," Jeremy huffed as they ran toward the doctor's office.

"We'll find out when we get back," Scot returned.

Minutes later, the boys returned with the doctor.

"Who's hurt?" he asked as they approached the caboose where the men had gathered.

Mr. Tyler stepped toward the doctor and explained, "Hank Fillmore was standing on the platform of the caboose watching as we went through the switch at the switchback and we bounced across a loose connector. He was thrown off the train."

"How bad's he hurt," Doc asked as he approached the car.

"I think it's his leg," Teddy replied. "I'm surprised he's not worse, but he seemed to know what he was doing and managed to control his fall."

"He did," Jeremy stated.

"What do you mean, Jeremy?" the man asked.

"He did?" the boy quickly changed his tone of voice.

Hank looked at the boy suspiciously, but didn't say anything as the doctor examined the damaged leg where he lay just inside the baggage door.

"It's a clean break," Doc explained. "Lower leg, but only one bone and it didn't break through the skin. We'll set it and splint it then get him to my office. I'll put a plaster cast on it to keep it in place so it can heal."

Doc Blevins set and splinted the leg while the boys went to his office to bring his carriage. The men lifted Hank into the carriage being careful to guide his leg to a safe position, then walked to the doctor's office to help get him inside and onto the examination table. Meanwhile, the train crew took the train to the sawmill to leave the loaded cars and pick up the empties. Once back in the company yard, they took the engine to service it and put it away for the weekend. Adam, Brett, and their pas stayed at Doc's to help get Hank back to the hotel once the doctor had finished treatment. Jay met them at the hotel when they returned with the patient. He had told Clara what had happened and she had a chair ready in the parlor with an ottoman in front on which to prop the injured leg.

After the two men and their sons left, the five gathered in the parlor. Clara brought the coffee pot and Jeremy the cups for the adults and Scot brought two glasses of milk for himself and his friend.

For a moment, nothing was said as each sipped on their drinks. Uncle Hank was the first to speak.

"Jeremy," he looked directly at the boy's eyes, "that was the second time you made a comment as though you know something we don't. What does it mean?"

Jay came to the boy's rescue. "Hank, we all know what Jeremy knows."

"Uncle Hank," the boy set his glass down. "How can such a nice man like you rob trains?"

"What!?" Hank sat bolt upright and almost tried to jump out of the chair.

"I saw you that day when you robbed the train and knocked Anthony on the head, then went out the back door and jumped from the train. You did that at Cripple Creek, too. That's how come you knew how to fall off the train today and not get yerself killed." He stood facing the man. "I think you're a great person and really do like you, but I don't understand." His voice cracked and he started to cry as he ran from the room.

Dumbfounded, the man stared at the boy as he left.

"We all care for you very much," Clara added. '

"Uncle Hank," Scot began. "We've suspected all along since the day of the robbery because Jeremy saw you get on the train with Mr. Easterly and his description of the train robber matched you."

Jay explained, "We caught Carson Easterly that same day because of Jeremy's warning that something didn't seem right. He's been in jail in

Arlee since and because of Jeremy's information and Scot's questions about your identity has been willing to help."

"You have known this all along?" the man asked in astonishment. "And still you have accepted me into your community?"

Scot continued, "Mr. Easterly said he got to thinking you weren't out so much to rob trains but found it an exciting challenge and that you hadn't spent any of the money."

"The railroad president, Mr. Marlow, knows all this and has hoped that by letting you stay on, it might prove to be true and he could get the judge to work out something helpful if the money, in fact, was returned." Jay worked on his coffee as he watched for the man's reaction.

Hank relaxed back into the chair and said nothing for a moment, but instead drank from his cup. He held the cup in his hands. "Obviously, I'm not going anywhere for the weeks it takes for my leg to heal." He looked at his nephew as he set the cup back on the table. "Scot, go up to my room and bring down my carpet bag."

The boy did as he was told and soon returned with the bag. Jeremy returned with him, rubbing the tears from his face. Scot handed the bag to his uncle.

"Jay," he reached into his bag, "put this in a safe place, I really don't need it any more." He handed the engineer his gunbelt and revolver.

"Wow!" Jeremy exclaimed, his still damp face beaming in wonder. "Is it loaded?"

"No, Boy. It never was."

Again, he reached into the bag and offered his nephew a key.

"Scot, this will open the trunk in the store room. All the money bags from the robberies are in there. That's all that's in there. You can give the trunk and the key to Mr. Marlow to do with as needed." The uncle reached once more for his coffee and drank with a much clearer conscience. "I feel much better. Carson was right. I feel so sorry for him. I never had the money I had promised him for his help. It really was an exciting adventure and I'm sorry I got caught up in it. And I'm grateful that it's over"

Jay drank his coffee as he listened to Hank and witnessed the exchange between him and his nephew. Emptying the cup, he set it aside.

"Hank Fillmore," he comforted. "I think you can relax and worry more about healing. You're right, you're not going anywhere. When I take tonight's train to Arlee, I'll make arrangements to see Mr. Marlow on Monday's run and for you to stay here until your leg mends. The chest and key will be turned over to him on Monday and he will get it back to Wells Fargo. When I return, I'll let you know what we do next."

Clara stood up with coffee pot in hand. "Refills?"

The men held out their cups. "Sure."

"Boys, let's go fix us some supper." She picked up her cup and turned to leave for the kitchen. "I'll fix trays so we can eat in here tonight."

The parlor clock struck the half hour past six.

"I'll get something at the Johnstons'. There's a train to take out and I have to go." He stood and grabbed his cap from where he'd left it on the side table. "Doc Blevins left a pair of crutches and they're in the kitchen. See you all tomorrow late morning." He followed Clara and the boys from the room.

From the hall, Scot was heard to tell Clara, "I'm going to stay in the parlor with Uncle Hank, if that's all right."

"Yes," Clara replied. "Jeremy and I can put things together for the four of us."

*　　*　　*

A damp and drizzling weekend slipped by. No one went anywhere other than Jay on his train run Sunday evening. The days were spent in the parlor where Hank could sit with his leg propped up. He shared stories about his life with his nephew and friends. Jeremy told of some of the pranks he'd played over the years. Scot told of life on the road with his pa. Jay shared some past history of the building of the logging company's rail lines into the mountains. Clara shared stories of the funny habits of some of her guests over the years. In between there were pots of coffee, glasses of milk, quiet time for reading, and an ongoing game of dominoes alongside Uncle Hank's chair so he could tell the boys where to put his domino pieces.

On Monday after early breakfast, the hotel's weekend guests checked out and were gone. At second breakfast all gathered in the kitchen as Hank opened the trunk so all could make sure the bank bags were accounted for. Scot helped Jay carry the heavy trunk to the station and place it in the baggage room on the train. The engineer kept the key in his pocket. Back at the hotel, the boys went to work helping Clara to clean the guest rooms. Jay went to Arlee. Once the rooms were clean and the linens gathered in the kitchen, the boys left for their jobs at the railroad and logging company. Clara and Hank kept each other company for the day, which began in the kitchen as the woman washed the bed linens and towels in the wash tub and hung them on the line in the hotel's back yard to dry. It was a day with warm sunshine and a light breeze, perfect laundry weather. After lunch, the two worked together to prepare the evening meal. Hank peeled and cut up potatoes and carrots to add to the roast Clara had prepared in its roasting pan. Hot coals were raked down and more wood added to the firebox and dinner was placed in the oven for a slow baking. While the roast cooked on the far side within the oven, the two mixed up and baked a batch of chocolate chip cookies in the side of the oven closest to the firebox. The warm aroma of delicious food permeated the kitchen and drifted down the hallway and into the other rooms. The day meandered lazily on until the quiet was ended by the return of the boys and the engineer.

"We're home!" the boys announced as they punctuated their arrival with the slamming of the front door and the clatter of boots down the wooden hallway. They kicked off their boots and hung their caps on the wall pegs as they gathered at the table with Uncle Hank.

"Cookies!" Jeremy shouted as he spotted a fresh batch resting on the cooling cloth on the side board.

"Wash up first," Clara instructed as she took a pitcher of milk from the ice box.

The boys paused for a quick hand washing at the sink, then hurried to return to the table. The woman set the milk on the table, then plated a dozen cookies and added them to the table. The boys each grabbed a glass from the middle of the table, poured themselves a glass of milk, then reached for a pair of cookies. Hank watched and waited, then helped himself as well. Clara took her seat and joined the others. In the quiet that followed, cookies and milk quickly disappeared.

"What took us hours is gone in a matter of minutes," the man observed.

"That's our boys," the woman added.

"They were good!" the boys concluded.

"Time to set the table," Clara announced as she removed the empty plate and glasses, then returned the milk to the ice box.

The front door swung open and Jay strode down the hall. "Smells delicious," he observed as he kicked off his boots and hung his engineer's cap on its peg. "Sheets are still blowing in the breeze."

"I totally forgot." The oven banged shut as Clara lifted out the roasting pan and set it on the warming plate to rest. "Will you boys bring in the linens, please," she asked.

"Yea," Scot replied as the two stuffed their feet into their boots and headed out the door.

"Was your meeting successful?" Hank asked.

"I'll tell all about it at supper. I'll go up and clean up." He turned down the hall toward the staircase. "But yes," he called over his shoulder.

The boys returned with the laundry basket and left it just inside the door, then proceeded to finish setting the table. Jay returned having washed up and changed out of his coveralls. Clara placed a cup of coffee on the table then turned her attention to plating the meal. The boys put the serving dishes on the table and all sat down to eat. Hank sliced the roast and passed the platter.

"How was your meeting with Mr. Marlow?" Scot asked as he helped himself to vegetables.

"As soon as I pulled in to Arlee, I had the freight agent assign two men to deliver the trunk to Mr. Marlow's office. I followed after the "King" was turned and serviced and the rain readied for the return trip." He helped himself to a slice of meet and took a sip of his coffee. "By the time I got to the president's office, he had sent for Melvin Harding, Wells Fargo's regional manager. I handed him the key and he opened the trunk."

"Your supper's getting cold," Hank observed. "We can wait till afterwards."

"Thanks."

The meal continued in quiet anticipation of the rest of the report after they retired to the parlor.

*　　*　　*

Jeremy carried a tray of cookies, Scot a tray of cups and glasses, and Clara a pitcher of milk and a pot of coffee. All was placed on a coffee table in the parlor. The boys tended the stove to stir up the heat and take off the chill of the day. Hank hobbled over to his chair and ottoman and lay the crutches on the floor at his side. The others settled on chair or sofa or floor, but not before taking a beverage and cookies from the coffee table.

"What happened next?" Uncle Hank asked.

Jay poured himself a cup of coffee and drank. He set the cup aside. "As I said, I gave Mr. Harding the key and he opened the trunk. The bank bags had not been opened and lay in the trunk as they had been when taken from the bank to the train. He opened the seal on one of the bags from a bank taken at Cripple Creek. The contents were untouched. 'I don't believe it.' He commented as Mr. Marlow and I looked on. 'Nothing's been touched.' Mr. Harding acknowledged.

"Mr. Marlow asked him how he wanted to handle it. I explained that you did it for the excitement and adventure. Mr. Harding said he wasn't sure what to do. Mr. Marlow asked if Wells Fargo wanted to press charges or was willing to take the money back without pressing charges. He shared that none of the baggage clerks had been seriously hurt and that many, including both the robber and his accomplice had helped to bring the matter to a close. The railroad wasn't going to press charges. Then he asked if Wells Fargo was offering a reward for those who helped to get the money returned.

"Yes, there was a reward and he handed Mr. Marlow $500.00. The man looked at the money in astonishment and remarked that this was very little considering that nearly a dozen people were involved in getting the money back. Mr. Harding reconsidered for a moment. Then he took another $6,000.00 from the bank bag and handed it to Mr. Marlow instructing that each person involved should receive $500.00. The bag was returned to the trunk and it was relocked. Mr. Harding put the key in his pocket and asked that the trunk be delivered to the Wells Fargo Bank where he would take care of getting each bank bag to where it belonged."

"What will happen to Mr. Easterly and my uncle?" Scot asked after swallowing a bite of cookie.

"I met with the Marshall and he was released. I took him to the hotel for breakfast, explained where your uncle is, gave him $500.00 of the reward money and offered a free ticket to come on out here with me. He said thanks, but he had to get on with his life and asked if a ticket to Pine Bluff would be okay. I gave him the ticket and he planned to leave on the northbound at midday."

"Thanks," Hank said as he finished his cup of coffee. "I sure wasn't any good for him and I'm glad he's on his own again with money in his pocket and hope he has some sort of plan." He reached for another cookie. Clara refilled his cup.

Jay finished a cookie and drank more of his coffee as he paused a moment before continuing. "I gave the Johnstons $1,500.00 for their family's support in all this and have the rest with me. There's $500.00 each for Anthony, Dan, Scott, and the five of us. That leaves the original

$500.00 reward money. I will tell Teddy and Bill how the logging company helped with this and let them do what they want with that money."

"I don't believe it," Hank sighed. "It's over, and I'm a free man with $500.00 to help me get started again." He finished his second cup of coffee and set the empty cup aside. "Now we can focus on finding Scot's pa."

Jeremy added, "And you have to get better, too."

"Thank you, Jeremy. I can work on that as well."

The parlor clock struck the hour at eight.

"I don't know about you all," Clara stood and picked up the coffee pot and milk pitcher. "But it's been a long day and I'm tired." She turned toward the door. "I want to put everything in the kitchen, go to bed, and clean up in the morning." She left the room.

"I agree," Jay said as he rose to his feet. "Why don't you boys take everything else to the kitchen then go to bed. I'll bank the fire for the night and take the light so Hank and I can go up for the night."

"Good night," each boy offered as he left the room with the trays of cups and glasses and the few remaining cookies.

The man rose from his chair and tended the stove, raking out the coals and adding two chunks of firewood, then adjusting the dampers down for the night. He picked up the kerosene lamb as Hank gathered his crutches and pushed himself out of the chair. The two left for the staircase and the room went dark as they departed.

*   *   *

A week later, Scot picked up two letters from the Well Fargo office. They bore a railroad post office postmark from Bismark in North Dakota Territory. One was addressed to him and one to Uncle Hank. When Jay brought the "King" in from the morning freight work, the boy told him of the letters. He also went to the car shop to let Jeremy know, and told each he was going home for lunch to give Uncle Hank his letter and to read his.

Entering the kitchen, Scot found the room empty and called out, "Where is everyone? I have letters!"

Hank hobbled in through the back door and held it open. Clara entered with am armload of firewood.

"You boys forgot the kitchen stove wood this morning." She dropped her load into the wood box. "What's all the excitement? And why are you home in the middle of the day?"

"I have letters!" the boy exclaimed.

All rushed to the table as he handed his uncle's to him and tore his own open and spread it on the table. He read aloud for all to hear.

4 May 1880
Cllint Robinson
Northern Pacific Railroad
Bismark, North Dakota Territory

My dear Scot,

I'm so sorry it has taken so long to get set up here and to begin to make arrangements for you to come out. Some years back the Northern Pacific Railroad ran into money problems and had to get reorganized before in could continue building. When I was suddenly sent out here back in March, they still didn't know what they were doing and I've had to wait while decisions were made. They have finally decided to start surveying a route west from here. I have a caboose for an office and place to live and store equipment and supplies. We can both live in it as I continue my work. The project manager has agreed that you are old enough to be my assistant and be hired as such by the railroad. Details have yet to be worked out. As soon as they are, I'll arrange for tickets for you and your uncle to make the trip out here.

I've written your uncle and your ma so she knows how to reach us.

I love you, Son, and can't wait until we're together again.

Your Pa

"Wow, he has no idea what you've been through," Clara remarked.

All looked up as the front door opened and Jay and Jeremy entered down the hallway. They quickly joined the three at the table. The woman poured a cup of coffee while Scot pushed a glass and the milk pitcher in the younger boy's direction.

Hank shared, "Scot just read his letter from his pa. This if mine."
Uncle Hank read his to all.

4 May 1880
Cllint Robinson
Northern Pacific Railroad
Bismark, North Dakota Territory

Hank,

I greatly appreciate you looking after my son while I find and get settled in my new assignment. I'll be working for the Northern Pacific Railroad as they get reorganized financially and begin to continue moving westward from Bismark to join up with construction in Washington Territory. I hope all has gone well for the two of you and that you have enjoyed getting to know each other better. I'm sorry for not being in touch with you personally, but the situation changed very suddenly and I had to go west before the two of you had gotten together. I sent Scot on to you alone because I had no other way to do so.

The situation here is still uncertain, so it will be some weeks yet until I can write again and send train fare for you both to join me out here.

Again, I am so grateful for your help in looking after my son.

Your brother-in-law,
Clint Robinson

Jeremy paused with cookie in hand. "Boy, he doesn't know what we've been doin'."

"Listen to Scot's letter. You are so right." Clara took a sip of her coffee. "Go ahead and read it again, Scot."

The boy reread his letter for the benefit of the newly arrived.

Jay swallowed his coffee and set the cup down. "Do we dare tell him what all has been happening here?" He reached for a cookie.

"I don't think he'll really want to know," Scot observed. "Everything is good now. We'll just write him about that. Maybe, someday, I'll tell him our story. But not now." He finished his glass of milk.

"It's good to see everyone in the middle of the day," Hank commented. "Thanks for bringing the letters, Scot, and for letting everyone know so we could share them together." He finished his coffee. "Can we do a quick lunch before everyone has to get back to work?"

"Come on, Boys," Clara pushed her chair back and stood up. "I have some soup to heat up and you two can put out the fixin's for sandwiches."

The letters were folded, returned to their envelops, and tucked away in shirt pockets as the table was reset for a quick lunch.

*　　*　　*

In the days that followed, life quietly slipped into a routine, but with variances. After early breakfast, Jay left for the morning passenger run to Arlee. The boys did their morning chores at the hotel, then left for their jobs at the station and the car shop. Uncle Hank did what he could to help around the hotel, but mostly sat while his leg began to mend. Generally on Wednesdays, the boys went up to work the day on the mountain with Brett and Adam. Going up they road in the caboose. When they returned in the evening on the train with Jay, they rode in the cab of the "Scott" and Scot began to operate the engine over portions of the route. Jeremy was allowed to serve as apprentice fireman and help feed the firebox. Brett and Scot generally stayed in the caboose with their pas. One trip was exceptional. Brett, having run the "Scott" the previous year, rode with them in the cab one trip and took the train in the entire trip. Friendships grew and extended into weekend fishing trips. One Friday was spent with Adam on his job at the "Herald" as all worked to get out the paper, including type setting and inking and printing. Evan Clancy, the owner of the paper, was very tolerant and enjoyed sharing his craft with the boys. The final edition showed the joy of the day with some pages wearing a little extra ink where it didn't belong. Scot continued to share correspondence with Jason as they sent occasional letters back and forth with Jay. As the weeks slipped away, May quietly drifted into early June.

*　　*　　*

At breakfast on the first Friday of June, Jay observed, "Hank, you seem to have mended quite well as you get around quite well with your crutches and spend less time parked in a chair. Am I right in this?" He worked on his eggs while he waited for a reply.

"I guess I am doing quite well, now," the man replied between forkfuls of fried potatoes.

"Would you and the boys be up for an overnight tonight?" he continued.

"You bet!" Jeremy cut in. Then he paused to look at Clara for her response.

"It's okay, Jeremy. Jay and I have already talked it over." She worked on her cup of coffee a moment. "You boys come home a half hour early from work this afternoon and get your chores done and extra wood in for Saturday morning, and you can take the Friday run with Jay this evening."

Scot finished a piece of toast then added, "Do the Johnstons know we're coming?"

"They do," Jay confirmed. "We're only spending the night, but there will be plenty to do the short time we are there." He turned his attention to his coffee.

"It'll be good to see Jason again and to watch the train activity, too." Scot finished his potatoes then drained his glass of orange juice.

"Will you be okay with this weekend's guests?" Jeremy asked, a piece of bacon on its way to his mouth.

"Uncle Hank and I will prepare the meals ahead of time so I can have all in readiness for tonight and tomorrow morning. I'll be fine, Jeremy. But thanks for asking." She drained her cup of coffee and stood to start clearing the table.

"I'll see you all tonight," Jay stated as he slipped into his boots, took his cap from its peg and headed to the door.

"Bye," the boys chorused.

"Have a good day," Clara added.

"Take care," Hank offered as he watched the man down the hall, then started passing food platters toward the end of the table.

*   *   *

The boys and Uncle Hank waited at the station with a single carpet bag containing their combined needs for the night. The platform area was alive with the activity of gathering passengers waiting for the "King" to take its place at the front of the train, positioned for its trip to Day's End. The boys and Hank knew many among the crowd from their days on the mountain. They were logging crew heading off for the weekend to visit friends or family elsewhere or just to have a good time in some distant town. Mr. Coates and his son, Jarrett, rolled the baggage wagon to the edge of the station platform and began to service the baggage end of the combine car. The boys and Hank worked their way to the car and visited as the father and son worked with the baggage clerk. The two finished and took the wagon back to the baggage room as the "King's" bell and whistle announced its arrival on the back side of the station.

The locomotive backed through the switches to pull up and couple to the end of the train, and await the time of departure. The man and two boys waved good-bye to the man and son as the two left, then turned toward the engine to climb into its cab.

"You boys can ride with Jay," Hank decided. "I don't think crutches are good for climbing to the cab. If it's all right with Anthony, I'll keep him company in the baggage room." He turned to the open platform in front of the locomotive and climbed aboard.

Scot and Jeremy climbed into the engine cab with its crew.

"You want to take us to Day's End, Scot," Jay offered.

"Are you sure?" the boy asked.

"I think you're ready." He motioned the boy to the engineer's seat. "I'm here if you need."

"All aboard!" Dan Seegers called from the coach steps as he boarded the train.

Scot reached for the whistle cord and let loose three short blasts as Scott started the bell to ringing and the boy shifted the Johnson bar into reverse and eased back on the throttle. The "King" responded in loud stately style and the train drifted out of the station. In smooth steady steps, the boy brought the train up to speed one click at a time, then locked the throttle to watch the track ahead from the window. Jeremy climbed to a seat on the wood pile in the tender.

"I'll watch the track, too," he announced as he settled in among the firewood.

"This is always the hardest part," Jay commented, "running in reverse to Day's End and watching the track around the tender." He looked up at the younger boy. "Thanks, Jeremy. Let us know if you see anything on the tracks."

The fireman fed the firebox, closed the door, and checked the gauges. He then crossed to the tender and opened the valve to add more water to the boiler as he watched the water glass rise to level, then shut the valve.

The routine run was interrupted by a shout from Jeremy. "Something on the tracks ahead!"

Scot slammed the throttle forward, pulled the Johnson bar into neutral, and applied the brakes. Steel screamed as sparks flew from brake shoes and wheels locked and screeched steel on steel as the train slowed to a sudden stop. Jay jumped down to run ahead and inspect the object on the track as the boys followed close behind to be joined by Dan and the two from the baggage room. Curious passengers stretched their heads out the windows to see what was happening. A small brown lump lying on the ties turned out to be a spotted fawn, curled up and fast asleep. It stirred as the people approached.

"Well I'll be!" the engineer exclaimed. "It slept through all this noise." He scanned the hillside for signs of a doe. "I wonder how it comes to be here all alone," the man pondered.

"Over here," Jeremy and gone ahead. "She's alive."

"Scot, stay with the fawn." The engineer went ahead to check on the doe the younger boy had discovered. "She's tangled in those vines, but seems to be okay."

The animal struggled without sound to try to free herself from the tangle of vines.

"Easy, Girl," Anthony soothed as he knelt by the mother. "I'll hold her, can someone untangle her legs?"

He cradled the frightened doe while Jay and Dan worked to untangle the vines from her legs. Once free, he released her and stepped back to give her room to get up.

The fawn stood with the other boy who turned her to face her mother. "There's yer ma, Little Feller. Go on to her." Scot gave the baby an encouraging shove as he guided it to its mother.

All watched as the little one took unsteady steps and advanced toward its mother, and stepped back to give the two room. The doe glanced at its audience then moved toward its fawn. Together once more, she nudged her child toward the wooded landscape beside the tracks. The two walked into the trees and disappeared. Back at the train, passengers watched out the windows as the drama played out, some pointing to focus their kids' attention. As the deer disappeared, folks settled back into their seats to await the trains' continued travel to Day's End. The train crew returned to their places on the train.

Scott stood on the footplate between the engine and its tender, and watched as everyone returned to the train. Suddenly he pointed toward the hillside beside the tracks. "Look!" he called.

All stopped and turned as he indicated, just in time to watch as a majestic buck crossed the tracks to follow the doe and her fawn into the wooded landscape beyond the train. Exclamations and pointing arms followed from coach windows as passengers caught sight of the vanishing buck.

"Thanks, Jeremy," Jay said as all gathered in the cab. "I don't know if we could have stopped in time if you hadn't seen the fawn in the track."

"I'll climb back up," the boy responded.

"Okay, Scot," the man turned to his trainee. "Let's go on."

Scot quickly put the train back into motion and brought it up to speed.

"This doesn't happen often," Jay commented. "But it does happen from time to time. We've had any number of encounters with various critters from wildlife to local livestock."

The balance of the trip was routine. Scot did the runaround to reconnect to the front end of the train and head back past Snow Shoe. The conductor shared that there were passengers to get off on the way by, so the train made a short stop at Snow Shoe station, then moved on. The boy's skills had improved and station stops were much kinder on folks with just the slightest last jerk at Kingston. The boy handed the engineer's seat back to Jay as they stopped for the switch onto the main line.

The train rolled into the station at Arlee. Jay stepped down from his seat and turned to Scott.

"Can you take it from here with Dan and the crew? I have to get these folks over to the hotel to get ready for dinner."

"Sure, Jay,"

To the boys he instructed, "Get your uncle and your travel bag and meet me at the bench by the station. I'll be right along."

Jeremy and Scot climbed down from the engine and went to the baggage room to get Uncle Hank and their carpet bag. Jay picked up his bag from where he kept it on the tender beside the wood load and followed close behind.

The four crossed the street to the hotel and, ignoring the activity in the lobby, went straight to Jay's room to change out of their travel and work clothes.

"Wash up and get dressed. Leave everything here until we get back, then we'll figure out where our rooms are."

He washed off the soot and changed into clean clothes while the boys did the same. Uncle Hank was fine as is.

"What's so special," Scot asked.

"We're to be picked up by carriage and taken to a special dinner." The man combed his hair and his beard as he checked his progress in the wash stand mirror. "This is something I think you once said you wanted before you have to leave."

"Oh?" He brushed his boots with his dirty shirt, then tossed it with his other clothes on the chair beside his carpet bag. He knocked the dirt from his cap and put it on. "I'm ready," Scot announced.

"Me, too," Jeremy chimed in.

Jason paused in the doorway.

"Hi, Jay," he greeted, "your carriage is here."

"Thanks, Jason. We'll be right down."

The older boy left.

"This must be something quite special," Hank observed.

"You'll see shortly," Jay replied.

The four descended the staircase to the lower hall into the front lobby. The crowd checking in had thinned, but Nancy and her son were still busy. "See you all when you get back," she called as they passed through the lobby.

Jay waved as they passed through. An open carriage with a passenger compartment behind the driver's bench stood waiting, pulled by a matched pair of grey mares. The four climbed aboard and took their seats. Hank leaned his crutches against his seat.

"Are you ready, Jay?" a familiar voice from the driver's seat asked.

"Yes, Charles," the engineer replied.

The carriage headed across the tracks and down the road toward the engine service yard. In the fading light of evening, the boys glanced up at the large shadow of the coal dock off to their right as they passed down the road that paralleled the engine service tracks. All was quiet as they moved along, then crossed the tracks to pass under the track above that fed into the top of the coal dock.

"I remember this track," Scot remarked as they turned up the back side of the coal dock. "This is where the president's car is stored." He looked ahead. "And there it is with lights on inside!"

Jay announced, "And this is the night you get to see it on the inside."

"Wow!" Jeremy whispered.

"Mr. Marlow asked me to bring you all to dinner with him tonight." He smiled to himself at the radiant grins of anticipation on the boys' faces.

"This is truly and honor," Hank said softly. "I robbed this man's trains and he invites me to dinner. I don't understand."

The carriage pulled up to a stop at the back steps to the car. A step stool awaited on the ground beside the car's steps.

"You folks go on up to the door. Mr. Marlow's expecting you." Howard stepped down from the front seat. "The carriage will be here until we return." He tied the reins to the hand rail beside the steps and walked toward the front of the car. "I'll have dinner in the kitchen with Howard and be ready when it's time to leave." He disappeared up the front steps.

The door opened and Philemon J. Marlow stood in the backlight from within. "Come on up, Folks. Hand me Hank's crutches so he has both hands for the railings."

The boys climbed the steps first and passed the crutches to the waiting host. Mr. Marlow took Hank's hand and pulled him up as Jay followed behind. Once inside, he invited all to sit wherever each chose in his parlor/office. As Hank and the boys settled on their cushioned seats, each gazed about the car at its stately interior. Rosewood and mahogany woods dressed the interior walls with furnishings of oak library shelving, cabinets, and desk with cushioned chairs and benches. Mr. Marlow settled in an oak swivel chair at this desk and turned to face his guests.

"Hank," he addressed the uncle. "I know this has been an unsettling time for you and am grateful for the return of the bank bags and in knowing you didn't intend to be a criminal, but must have had some exciting times."

"Sir, I didn't have anything else to do at the time and thought it might be quite the adventure. I'm surely sorry for the trouble I caused and relieved that it's over. And truly delighted to have had time with my nephew." He shifted in his chair to get his leg into a more comfortable position. "This Jeremy kid's quite something, too."

The younger boy sat forward on his chair. "Things haven't been so boring since you came along," he volunteered. "I've sure had fun."

Howard entered from the front hall. "Dinner's on the table, Sir. I placed Scot with his uncle, Jeremy with you, and Hank in a chair at the end of the table where he can put his crutches on the floor."

"Thanks, Howard." He stood and followed his steward into the hall. All followed.

*   *   *

It was close to eight-thirty by the time all gathered in the kitchen at the hotel for coffee, milk, and cake. The four shared with the Johnstons their evening with Mr. Marlow and the adventure of the trip from Snow Shoe.

"That's some fancy car!" Jeremy exclaimed between mouthfuls of cake.

"That was some fancy dinner," Hank added. "Prime rib with all the fixin's, as well as wine and sasparilla for the boys, and finished off with strawberry pie with ice cream on top!"

Scot cut in, "He even gave us a tour of his car, and before we left, a tour of his parlor car!" He sipped on his milk, then turned his attention to the cake.

Jason set his glass down. "Well, Jay, I guess this has been quite an evening. You all came just for this, didn't you?"

"I met with Mr. Marlow last week and asked him if he thought this could work out." He drank from his coffee. "He said to bring them in on tonight's run and we'd make an evening of it." Turning to Hank and the boys he continued, "I guess you all enjoyed it?"

"We sure did!" Scot confirmed. "This was real special." He finished his cake and emptied his glass.

Hank Johnston set his empty cup on the table. "We put the boys in Jason's room for the night and Uncle Hank in with Jay," he instructed. "We'll all be up early tomorrow for the train back, so we might do a quick cleanup then head off to bed."

"Thanks," Uncle Hank acknowledged as he stood with his crutches and maneuvered toward the hall.

"Good night," the boys chorused as they placed their dirty dishes on the side board.

"See you in the mornin'," Jay followed the boys out.

"Night, Ma," Jason departed.

The light in the kitchen dimmed as each took a light to see their way to their rooms. The last of the dishes and food were put away and the Johnstons took the last light to their room off the hall, just outside the kitchen.

The room went dark.

*   *   *

Jason crossed the station platform with Jay and his guests as the engineer went ahead to prepare his train for departure. Scott Donaldson had already built up the fire in the firebox and brought the engine up to steam pressure. As departure time drew nearer, passengers arrived and the baggage wagon was drawn up to the baggage door to load outgoing packages and mail. Jay motioned for the boys to come up to the cab and Jason said his farewells. Hank hobbled over to the baggage end of the combine while his nephew and young friend climbed up with the engine crew. Commotion dwindled as passengers boarded and the baggage wagon was pulled away. Hank waved to the boy on the platform from the baggage room door before Anthony rolled the door closed. All waved from the engine as the conductor cleared the train to leave. Jay sounded the whistle as Scott started the bell in its rhythmic ringing. Steam rushed into the piston chambers and the rods began to push the wheels into motion. Couplings rattled taught. The train eased out of the station. The lone boy on the platform watched it out of sight, then turned to return home and to morning chores.

The train streaked through the sun-drenched countryside on its routine Saturday morning run. Passing through Blakesville and Kingston, it slowed for the bridge and Chamber's Crossing to pick up Jamie, then moved on to its stop at Snow Shoe. Scot Robinson was in his element, having taken the throttle from the moment the train cleared the switch off the main line. He took the train on to Day's End, did the run-around, then returned to the track behind the station. There, the coach cars were dropped for the rest of the weekend and the boy took the "King" and turned it on the wye track, then proceeded to the wood pile and the water tank to be serviced, then across the ash pit to dump its fire, then into the engine house to sleep until Sunday evening.

*   *   *

Life's daily routine changed in the middle of the following week with the arrival of two new letters. All gathered in the hotel kitchen for noon meal while Scot and Uncle Hank read their letters. Clara placed the coffee pot and a pitcher of milk in the middle of the table while Jeremy plated cookies from the cookie jar and added it.

Scot poured himself a glass of milk and began on a cookie as he offered, "Uncle Hank, why don't you go first. Pa's most likely to have what we're to do in your letter."

The man tore open the end of his envelop and withdrew the paper from within.

3 June 1880
Cllint Robinson
Northern Pacific Railroad
Bismark, North Dakota Territory

Hank,

I have finally found a stable situation with the railroad's plans to build west from Bismark. As I wrote earlier, I have been given a caboose as an office and residence until the construction project is completed. Scot can live with me in the caboose and help with my surveying work as we go forward.

For the foreseeable months, much will be planning and some travel west to explore possible routes and sketch preliminary maps for further review. We will live in the caboose as our home base, but have to do exploratory travel by horse and pack animal, or when possible, by wagon. But we will be together again.

I've enclosed a packet of $50.00 bank checks from Wells Fargo, made out to you to cash as you need for train fare and supplies along the way. As far as I know, you can travel by train all the way to Bismark and Wells Fargo has banks and agents along the way. Please start as soon as you are able.

Again, I am so grateful for your help in looking after my son.

Your brother-in-law,
Clint Robinson

Hank finished reading his letter and all sat in silence as they digested its contents.

"This feels so sudden," Scot remarked as he tore open his own letter.

The boy spread his letter on the table as he munched on his cookie, then began to read.

3 June 1880
Cllint Robinson
Northern Pacific Railroad
Bismark, North Dakota Territory

My dearest son,

I long to see you again and hope you have been enjoying your time with your uncle, and can't wait for you to tell me of all your adventures and the people you have met. It has been so hard not knowing what has happened to you and what you have been doing.

As I wrote in his letter, I have finally been able to settle down in a situation that will allow you to join me as soon as you are able to journey west. Your uncle has money and instructions on how to get tickets and travel by train.

I love you, Son, and can't wait until we're together again.

Your Pa

The boy sat in silence as he drank from his glass of milk. "This feels so sudden," Scot repeated flatly. "I'm not ready. I don't want to leave here!" His voice broke. "It's become home and you all have become family." He choked up and the tears began to sting his eyes. He wiped them away with the back of his hand, then buried his face in his arms on the table and began to cry uncontrollably.

Uncle Hank swallowed hard to hold back his emotions and closed his eyes tightly to hold back the tears. It was no use. Emotion contorted his face as he fought for control, but he finally had to relax and let the tears flow.

Clara and Jay felt the emotion as their eyes moistened and they wiped away the tears. At first, Jeremy stared in disbelief as he didn't quite comprehend what the contents of the letters meant.

Suddenly, Scot's words sank in – "I don't want to leave here." And he knew. The sudden pain of reality flashed across his face as he flew into the woman's arms and burst into uncontrollable sobs. "He..can't..go," the boy cried as he held tight and the woman pulled him into her lap and tried to comfort him.

The flow of emotion lasted for a long time as each sank into his own personal conflict. As much as all had looked forward to the letters from Scot's pa, no one was ready for the reality of what must follow.

*　　*　　*

Life changed. Hank continued to navigate about on his crutches. Doc Blevins had seen him on a follow up visit and confirmed his progress was good. But he still had weeks to go before the plaster could come off. He wrote out a set of instructions for whomever might be found as a doctor in the West. Jay checked with Mr. Marlow as to the disposition of the trunk that had held the bank bags and found that it could be returned to Hank. It arrived on the train by week's end. Some of the reward money was used to buy clothing for the man and his nephew to be more appropriate for the western climate and culture and to carry through the summer and into the winter ahead. The two began to pack the trunk as clothing and materials were acquired. It was determined that they would not rush their departure, but plan for the following week's end when Jay would take the Friday train to Arlee and they would have a final visit with the Johnstons. Scot and Uncle Hank wrote a joint letter to Clint to inform him of their plans and give him an idea of when to expect their arrival in Bismark. Scot was sorry he hadn't replied to his Pa's first letter, it didn't occur to him at the time and it was too late now. He would share his time in Snow Shoe with his pa when they were together again. Hank cashed the first two of the checks at the bank and went with Jay to meet with Robert Coates to acquire tickets as far west as he could arrange. They managed passage through Truckee and west as far as the Baltimore and Ohio Railroad could take them. Ephram wired the agent in Bismark to request whatever official documents could be sent from the offices of the Northern Pacific Railroad to instruct Hank and railroads along the way as to what transfers were needed and ticketing from one to another.

By Monday evening of their last week together, progress was nearly complete. The boys and Uncle Hank had begun their game of dominoes when Clara and Jay entered the parlor with their cups of coffee. They settled in chair and sofa and watched the game for a while.

"Your games have gone much faster," Clara observed as she sipped from her cup.

Jeremy put his piece in the lineup and looked at the woman to reply, "We've been playing so much, we almost see our match ends before we put our pieces down and can place them very quickly as soon as the domino is placed in front." As if to emphasize the truth of the statement, the three played two rounds of placements in one smooth piece by piece motion.

"I see what you mean," Jay noted. He paused to drink from his coffee, then set the cup on the side table. He stood and left the room.

The others watched him go, then returned to their game. Clara continued to watch the game as she sipped on her coffee.

Moments later, the man returned. He carried Hank's gun belt. "Hank," he began. "I really have no need for this and truly believe you might need it where you two are going. Just in case, I wish you would add it to your trunk. I realize you have no bullets for it and suggest you stop at Jenkin's Store tomorrow and purchase a couple boxes – just in case."

Looking up from the game, Hank replied, "Leave it on the table for now and I'll put it in the trunk when we go up to bed." He turned his attention back to the game.

"I wish we could all go," Jeremy remarked.

"I know," Scot acknowledged. "Maybe we could get in the habit of writing letters. I'm sure not good at it, didn't even write my pa." It was quiet as they placed three quick rounds of domino pieces.

Clara broke the silence. "I will help Jeremy to sit down at the kitchen table and write to you, Scot, if you'll write back."

"Would you, Scot? Would you write to me?" He held his next piece in anticipation of his friend's reply.

Before picking up his next piece, the older boy looked to his young friend. "I'll sure try, Jeremy. I hope I can make myself write. It's gonna be a tough habit ta make." He reached for another domino.

The younger boy's face betrayed his disappointment in the vagueness of the reply.

Hank added his thoughts. "Scot, I'll be sure your pa knows you have a responsibility to keep in touch with Jeremy and that he has Jeremy's address so you have no excuse."

Jeremy smiled in appreciation. Scot frowned.

The parlor clock struck the half hour past eight.

"Time for bed," Jay shared. He finished his coffee and stood to take the cup to the kitchen. Clara followed.

"Game's done," Scot announced as he helped pack the pieces back in their boxes.

Hank reached for his crutches. "Scot," he asked, "could you please bring the gun to the trunk?"

The boy stood and stretched tired muscles. "Sure, Uncle Hank." He picked up the gun belt on his way to the door.

Jeremy placed the game boxes on the shelf and picked up his lamp. "Follow me, Uncle Hank," he instructed as he left the room.

Scot picked up the last lamp and waited in the hallway for Jay to return from the kitchen. The hotel darkened as Clara took her lamp from the kitchen to her bedroom and Scot led the way up the staircase with Jay close behind.

*   *   *

For the balance of the week, life followed its past routine as though nothing special lay ahead. The boys spent Wednesday on the mountain and said their farewells to the friends of the past weeks. Scot enjoyed one last day working with Adam on his pa's crew and a solemn mood prevailed as the day ended and they left on the last train. Jeremy shared that even though Scot was leaving, he hoped he could continue spending Wednesdays working with Brett and Horace. In the back of their minds, each knew it was their last time together, and they treasured every moment.

All too soon, Friday morning dawned, with a brilliant sun on the eastern horizon. Clara and the boys started early on a lavish breakfast of hot cakes and sausage with scrambled eggs and donuts. Clara had purchased a picnic basket from the general store with hinged wooden covers at each end. She had also purchased new cloth napkins to use to pack extra food for the start of the journey, and two travel tin canisters for coffee and milk along with a pair of tin cups to carry in the basket with the food.

Following breakfast, all worked together to pack the extra food. Pancakes and sausages were wrapped in the cloths along with several donuts. The pancakes were small enough to roll around a sausage for a drip free meal. A dozen cookies were added for good measure. All was covered with a clean towel and the two cups placed inside and on top of the food.

The trunk had been carried over to the station, tagged with travel information, and placed on the baggage wagon the night before. A single carpet bag carried clothing and necessities for overnight stays along the way, though it was likely some nights would be spent sleeping on the train. Scot and Hank took one last longing glance around the kitchen that had become such an integral part of their daily lives, and now, would be lost forever. Each felt a painful knot in his stomach as the reality set in.

"It's time to go," Jay announced as he picked up the two canisters. Clara took charge of the food basket as Scot took up the carpet bag. Hank had his hands full with his crutches as he hobbled down the hallway in front of the woman and small boy.

The party crossed the street to the train station and paused on the platform starring at the waiting train. Each set his burden down on the wooden platform. Surrounded by the noise of gathering passengers, reality slammed hard with devastating consequences.

Jeremy gazed at the train, then turned toward Scot.

"I..don't..want..you.to..go," Jeremy sobbed uncontrollably as he stood before his friend, wringing his hands in emotional distress.

Scot knelt in front his young friend and before he could reach out to him, Jeremy rushed into a panicked embrace, wrapping his arms around the older boy's neck and pulling tightly. Scot wrapped his young friend in a gentle and loving embrace as the two held each other in a brief eternity of pain.

"Jeremy," he sobbed, "I wish I didn't have to go either, and that my pa could come here and we could stay. But it's not gonna happen."

He stood up and lifted the small figure from the wooden platform, shifting his arms to support the weight. The two stood there, locked together in the pain of parting, tears dampening each other's shoulders.

Those standing nearby couldn't help but to feel the pain the boys shared, and the flood of silent tears increased.

"I will never forget you, Jeremy," Scot whispered in choked voice. "I will always cherish the memory of my time here in Snow Shoe with you and Clara and Jay and the people of the railroad and Stewart Creek." He emphasized each point with jolts of increased tightness in his embrace.

Hank turned a tearful face towards Jay and reached out a hand in farewell. The engineer responded by grabbing the hand and pulling the man into a farewell embrace of their own. Clara looked on in forlorn grief and was quickly pulled into a group embrace as Hank reached an arm in her direction. The crutches clattered to the wooden deck. The moment was brief, but felt like forever. All knew that it was. Once Scot and Uncle Hank boarded the train, they would never see each other again.

The boys relaxed and Scot set his friend back down on his own feet. But they couldn't let go. The older boy continued to wrap his arms around the shoulders, heaving with emotion, and rest his chin in the mass of blond hair, and the younger to embrace his friend around the waist. The tears continued to flow.

As the adults regained their composure, Hank recovered his crutches and stepped up beside the boys and placed a hand on Jeremy's shoulder. The small boy immediately released his friend and turned to embrace the uncle who responded with an emotional embrace of his own.

"I love you, Uncle Hank," he sobbed, somewhat more controlled. He looked up into the man's face. "I know you have to go, but I sure wish you didn't." The tears ran down his cheeks and dripped from his chin.

The man couldn't control his own grief of the moment at the sight of the boy's flood of tears, and couldn't speak. Finally, he responded, "Jeremy, you and Clara and Jay are the best thing that ever happened to me in my life." He knelt and rested his chin in the abundance of blond hair, thoroughly dampened with Scot's tears. "For the first time in my life, I belonged somewhere with people who mattered. My nephew and you folks gave my life purpose." He shifted his embrace to hold the boy by the shoulders as he remained kneeling before him. "I, too, will never forget my time here. I have no idea what lays ahead for me. Once we get to Bismark and Scot's pa, my purpose in life will end and I will have to start all over again. Perhaps I will return, perhaps not. I really don't know." He stood to face Jay and Clara. "This I do know. Whatever I do will be affected by what has happened here in these past few weeks. I'm no longer the man I was, and for that, am so grateful to the three of you."

"Hank," Clara began. "It has been such an adventure having you in our lives."

"You will definitely be missed, both of you," Jay added.

Scot walked over to his engineer friend. "Jay." He couldn't say anything more. The man sensed his grief and drew him close in a heartfelt embrace, and the tears flowed once more. They held each the other tightly as they cried uncontrollably in the knowledge that this parting was forever; knowing, too, how close they had become, the temporary bond of father and son. "Oh, I so wish I didn't have to go," he finally managed. "I love you like a second pa. And it hurts so!" Again, a new flood of tears. The embrace grew tighter. Jay shifted his hold to the boy's shoulders and held him at arm's length.

"I love you, too, Son. It won't be too many days more and you will be reunited with your pa and the two of you can get on with your lives again." He pulled the boy into one last brief embrace, then stood apart. "These past few weeks will become a memory, a very treasured memory, for us all. I really hate to say it, but I have a train to run and you a trip to make." The man pulled his kerchief from his pocket, blew his nose, and wiped the tears from his face.

In the mean time, the station platform cleared as the passengers, oblivious to the painful drama that unfolded in their midst, boarded the train with friends standing outside the cars visiting their last from below the windows. Quiet began to settle.

The engineer walked toward his locomotive and a train crew with dampened eyes, who had witnessed the profound grief of parting.

Clara, Hank, and the boys stood silently and watched him leave. As Jay climbed the steps to the engine's cab, he never looked back. He couldn't. There was too much pain.

"Should we get you two on the train?" Clara asked.

"We should," Hank replied. "But, if Scot's okay with it, we could have a brief more time and take it on the way back from Day's End."

"Yes!" Jeremy exclaimed.

"Are you sure?" the woman asked. "It will just prolong the pain."

"I think so," Scot put in. "Maybe it will be easier now that we've shared our feelings." He started toward the train. "I'll tell Dan."

The boy met briefly with the conductor and arranged for the train to pause on its way back to pick them up. Dan waved the "all aboard" and the train eased into reverse and soon cleared the station. The last of the friends of those on the train left the area. An intense silence remained.

"What now?" the woman asked.

"A cup of coffee in the waiting room?" Scot suggested.

"Me, too?" Jeremy asked.

"You, too," Clara confirmed.

The four left the travel bag, lunch basket, and canisters on the station platform and crossed the wooden deck to the station room.

ABOUT THE AUTHOR
J. ARTHUR MOORE

J. Arthur Moore is an educator with 42 years experience in public, private, and independent settings. He is also an amateur photographer and has illustrated his works with his own photographs. In addition to **Stranded in Snow Shoe**, Mr. Moore has written **Twelfth Winter; Journey into Darkness**, a story in four parts, **Blake's Story**, Revenge and Forgiveness, two Civil War historic fictions; and **Summer of Two Worlds**, a Native American historic fiction set in Montana Territory in the summer of 1882. **Twelfth Winter** is the sequel to **Summer of Two Worlds** and tells the story of Prairie Cub after he is forced to return to the world of his white heritage, the world of his former name, Michael. It is the emotional journey that followed. **Stranded in Snow Shoe** is the prequel, the story of the friend who set the stage for **Twelfth Winter**.

He recently published a third Civil War era historic fiction, **West to Freedom**. An earlier recent work, **Summer at Stewart Creek**, is pure fiction, set in the fictitious territory of his Virginia and Truckee Railroad of West Virginia, which he has recreated in miniature and used to illustrate this story. It is the same world in which Michael finds himself, and the beginning of the Virginia & Truckee Railroad collection of which *Summer of Two Worlds* trilogy is a part.

A graduate of Jenkintown High School, just outside of Philadelphia, Pennsylvania, Moore attended West Chester State College, currently West Chester University. Upon graduation, he joined the Navy and was stationed in Norfolk, Virginia, where he met his wife to be, a widow with four children. Once discharged from the service, he moved to Coatesville, Pennsylvania, began his teaching career, married and brought his new family to live in a 300-year-old farm house in which the children grew up and married, went their own ways, raised their families to become grandparents themselves.

Retiring after a 42-year career, Mr. Moore has moved to the farming country in Lancaster County, Pennsylvania, where he plans to enjoy the generations of family, time with his model railroad, and time to guide his writings into a new life through publication. It also allows for the opportunity to participate in a local model railroad club as well as time for traveling to Civil War events, and presenting at various organizations and events about the boys who were part of that war. He also shares the process of writing, and readings from his work, and does book signings at a variety of locations.

Mr. Moore can be reached through the contact page of the website for his books at **www.jarthurmoore.com** with links to his Facebook and Twitter pages; and a blog page focusing on the stories of the boys who served in the Civil War.

OTHER BOOKS BY
J. ARTHUR MOORE

These books by J. Arthur Moore are also available on
www.jarthurmoore.com and from the publisher, Omnibook Company
at www.omnibookcompany.com/journeyintodarkness/ as well as
www.barnesandnoble.com, and www.amazon.com
Also available from Ingram Distribution
[Ingram new accounts 1-800-937-0152]

Omnibook titles may be purchased in bulk for educational, business,
fund-raising, or sales promotional use. For more information
please e-mail info@omnibookcompany.com